FRIEND OR FOE?

The riders were coming up to Clint in a rush. They swarmed around him like giant insects and hardly even slowed down before sweeping him up along with them. Of course, it helped that Clint had been planning on being swept away from the moment he'd fired that shot over the other man's head.

"And who the hell are you?" the man asked while giving Clint a thorough once-over.

"Funny. I was about to ask you the same question."

"I'm after that man you were talking to a moment ago."

"Talking to?" Clint said. "I was letting my gun do most of my talking for me."

Clint could feel the hunger for blood hanging in the air over the other riders like a foul-smelling cloud that followed their every move. For that reason, he rode to the head of the pack until he was next to the older man in the lead.

"Damn!" snarled the silver-haired man. "That bastard's about to get around that ridge."

"Good thing I came along then," Clint said. "Because I know where he's headed."

The older man looked him over and nodded as a smile grew across his face. "Welcome aboard, son. You just officially joined this posse."

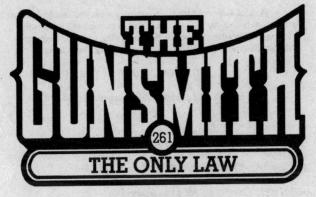

THE GUNSMITH

261

THE ONLY LAW

J. R. ROBERTS

JOVE BOOKS, NEW YORK

THE ONLY LAW

A Jove Book / published by arrangement with
the author

PRINTING HISTORY
Jove edition / September 2003

ISBN: 0-515-13600-X

A JOVE BOOK®
Jove Books are published by The Berkley Publishing Group,
a division of Penguin Group (USA) Inc.,
375 Hudson Street, New York, New York 10014.
JOVE and the "J" design
are trademarks belonging to Penguin Group (USA) Inc.

PRINTED IN THE UNITED STATES OF AMERICA

10 9 8 7 6 5 4 3 2 1

ONE

It always seemed as though the wind had a special way of blowing depending on certain times of the day or year. Not only were there changes because of weather, but the breezes actually took on a different voice when there were different things to be expressed.

An autumn wind was different than a summer one for more reasons than hot or cold or any storms that were passing through. The difference gave each season a different flavor that could be felt on more levels than just a chill or humid heat. Sometimes, the wind seemed to call out as it rolled over the land, shaking the branches and stirring up whatever it could along the way.

At times like those, it was easier to believe in things that a man couldn't exactly see or feel. Even a fellow without much religion in his heart found it easier to look up with the expectation that someone up there was looking back down at him. When the wind blew just the right way at certain times of the day, it sent more than a chill through folks' bones. Some Indians said it was spirits talking, while superstitious gamblers said it was lady luck giving them a bad sign. Most others didn't have a proper name for it, but the wind talked to them all the same.

After all, it was hard not to listen when something so loud was breathing down your neck from all sides.

City folk weren't so quick to believe in such things. A person had to live out in the open country for a while to appreciate things like all the different kinds of wind. A small town would do as well, since there weren't enough buildings to block out such things as runaway gusts that rattled windows in their panes and shook doors upon their hinges.

It was easy to shrug off such things as these when someone lived in New York City or San Francisco. For most people out on the prairie, it was a different story. And for folks who lived in states like Montana, where the trees and open range stretched out around them for what seemed like forever in every direction, it was even easier.

Clint Adams wasn't normally the type of man to let such things as ghost stories and noisy gusts of wind rattle him in the least. He'd seen enough wickedness in the world that he didn't have any more room left for superstition. But Clint Adams was also a gambler at heart. He might not have made his living by playing cards, but any man who was forced to keep his gun at his side nearly every waking moment had to have a gambler inside his soul.

No matter how quick his hand was or how confident he was in the steel at his side, Clint Adams knew damn well that every time the lead started to fly it was a gamble. Just like in any game of chance, everyone got lucky sometimes. The best poker player had his off days, and the sun, as the saying went, would even sometimes shine on a dog's ass.

It was that gambler inside Clint's soul that made him sit up and take notice when he heard what could only be an ill-tempered wind. The kind of gust that seemed to knock on the walls like an angry giant demanding entrance. Sounds like that stirred something primordial within Clint's gut and made him instinctively want to head somewhere with better cover.

"What was that?"

The words came from a slender woman with long, dark blond hair. Her skin was tanned and seemed especially so considering the time of the year. Her blue eyes were wide as they flicked toward the window which even now still shook in its frame, as if it was about to shatter at any second.

Her face had a natural beauty to it even though her nose was a little on the big side. Full, soft lips parted slightly to allow the tip of her tongue to dart out for a moment just to wet them. The blonde's body was trim and her pert little breasts were firm, capped by small, erect nipples. Long, willowy arms draped down so her hands could rest upon Clint Adams's bare chest, and her equally long legs were wrapped around Clint's waist.

Clint wasn't facing the window, but he could almost feel the glass shaking behind him as the intense wind assaulted the side of his hotel room. Straining his neck so he could try to look over his shoulder, Clint felt the blonde's body tense on top of him. His hands were already on her hips, so he tightened his grip slightly to keep her in place.

"It was just the wind, Adriana," Clint said. "Nothing to get spooked over."

Adriana pulled in a breath and looked away from the window, turning her gaze back to look Clint in the eyes. She smiled and lowered her head so that her hair spilled down to close them in.

Even though Clint had felt some of the same uneasiness, that feeling disappeared once he could see nothing but her and was surrounded by the blonde's sweet scent. He was sitting in an old rocking chair in the hotel room he'd rented for the night. He didn't know the proper name of the town he was in and didn't really care since it was simply a place to spend the night.

Having pulled in on a stage headed east to the Dakota Territories, Adriana was merely passing through as well. Her path crossed Clint's outside a run-down restaurant that served nothing but gristly meat and stale rolls, and that same path eventually led to Clint's hotel room.

Clint sat in the rocker with Adriana on his lap, her legs wrapped around him and snaking through gaps in the wooden rods that formed the back of the chair. Their naked bodies were pressed together and had been moving as one right up to the point when it seemed as though the wind was going to knock over the entire hotel.

"I swear I heard more than the wind out there, Clint."

Clint was moving his hands over her hips and down along the firm curve of her buttocks. Adriana's muscles were tensed just from keeping on top of him, and when she tensed slightly, she closed in even tighter around him.

Clint felt himself growing harder inside of her, and the outside world quickly began to lose its appeal. "There could be a storm coming," he said. "Or maybe it's just the time of year. I nearly got knocked out of my saddle on the way into town, so don't worry about it."

She really seemed to focus on him then and leaned forward to press her lips against his. They were still warm from the last time she'd kissed him, and their tongues caressed each other with the same amount of passion as Clint's hands roaming over her body.

Pulling away slightly, she nodded and said, "You're right. I'm just not used to this anymore after living out west for so long."

"You used to live in these parts?" Clint asked, sensing that she was relaxing once again, but wasn't quite as relaxed as before.

"Yes, in this town actually, but I don't want to think

about that. I'd rather think about what I'm doing right here and right now."

With that, Adriana slipped her hands around the back of Clint's neck and pulled herself up an inch or so. That was just enough for her to grind along the stiff shaft of his penis before lowering herself down once again. As Clint slid all the way inside of her, she leaned her head back and let out a contented moan.

Clint guided her with his hands on Adriana's hips. He leaned back as well, feeling the chair rock slightly as she commenced the rhythm they'd been building before getting distracted.

It still sounded like a storm was forming right around the very center of the hotel. The wind howled like a banshee and pounded angrily upon the outside of the building. There were other sounds as well, but Clint couldn't hear them over the sound of Adriana's slowly building moans.

TWO

As Adriana slid all the way down Clint's length, she groaned at the back of her throat, digging her fingernails into Clint's shoulders until he was all the way inside of her. Her slender body was stretched out in front of him as she leaned back as far as her arms would allow. The motion caused the rocking chair to creak forward until she felt as though she might fall out.

But Clint wasn't about to let that happen. As they both moved forward, he slid one hand up along her back to support her. The other hand stayed on her hip at first, but slowly moved up to the base of her spine. From there, he could feel the movement of her body a split second before she made it. Her muscles tensed beneath her skin as she began pumping her hips back and forth against him.

Her vagina clenched around his shaft just before she pulled herself back into an upright position. Keeping one hand on his shoulder, she looked into Clint's eyes to see his reaction to the tight wetness between her legs. She smiled, while baring some teeth like a hungry animal. With her other hand, Adriana drew a line between her breasts, over her firm stomach and down to the nub of sensitive flesh between her legs.

6

She struggled to keep her eyes open as her fingertips slipped through the dark hair. Once she found her clitoris, Adriana sucked in a deep breath and clenched once more around him before sliding her fingers back up along her stomach.

Watching that, Clint felt the pleasure well up inside of him until he thought he was going to burst. That struggle only added to the passion, however, as he took firm hold of her buttocks and shifted his weight so the rocker tipped back in his direction. On top of him, Adriana tensed for a moment until she regained her balance.

Clint thrust his hips forward and pulled her to him, burying his cock deep inside her body. He made sure to shift her as well so that he rubbed against her in the same place that she had rubbed herself as he slid inside. By the time the rocker had tilted back as far as it was going to go, Adriana had wrapped both arms around Clint and pressed herself as tightly as possible against him. She pumped her hips back and forth in time with his, burying her face against his neck as he thrust again and again along that spot she'd invited him to go.

The rocker had been placed next to the bed, with its back to the hotel room's only window. With both of them leaning in the same direction, the chair tipped all the way back, until it knocked against the bottom of the windowsill. Adriana didn't waste a single moment before taking hold of the windowsill and using it to brace herself as she ground against Clint's body while he pumped between her legs.

Clint could feel her breath hot against his cheek even after Adriana lifted herself up so she could look down at him. She had both hands on the sill now and was shifting her feet so her heels were propped against the edge of the rocker's seat. All Clint had to do was move his head forward a bit and he could take one of her nipples into his mouth.

Even though the chair was locked in place, Adriana was still rocking with full force on top of him. She used the muscles of her back and abdomen in turn to ride along Clint's penis, taking it inside of her again and again. Each time she dropped down a little harder, until beads of sweat began to slip over her skin.

Using his hands to keep her on top of him, Clint held onto Adriana while flicking his tongue over her breasts. The blonde's curves were slim yet succulent and her nipples felt like warm candies on his lips. When he nibbled here and there, he could hear Adriana squeal and giggle at the same time. The chair was knocking against the windowsill so hard by that point that it all but drowned out the sound of the wind which still raged outside.

As his hands slid over the tight curve of her backside, Clint was taken over by an urge he had no intention of holding back. It took some doing, but after a bit of wrangling, he managed to get up and off the chair. Adriana had locked her arms and legs around him, making it a little easier to lift them both from their spot.

Just as she was going to ask what he was doing, she was being set back down, onto the floor, and turned around so that she was facing the window. Clint's hands moved along her sides before creeping around to cup her breasts. She fit inside his grasp perfectly, with just a little room to spare.

Clint moved so that he could kiss the side of her neck while firmly massaging her soft flesh. Every so often, he took a nipple between thumb and forefinger, applying just enough pressure to send a ripple through Adriana's body. His hard cock was pressed against her backside, and she spread her legs just enough for him to feel the hot dampness of her pussy.

Without warning, Clint took hold of her and lifted Adriana off the floor. She was thinking the same thing he was, since she had already bent her knees, which allowed

Clint to set her back down upon the rocker. This time, she was facing the opposite direction with one hand on the back of the chair, the other hand on the windowsill and her knees on the wooden seat.

She pressed her chest against the chair and arched her back, spreading her legs as Clint slid in between them. Craning her head back, she smiled widely as she felt Clint's hands moving over her body and keeping her steady.

Clint moved his cock between her thighs and entered her from behind. The chair put Adriana at just the right height for him to slide into her with ease. Once he was inside, Clint grabbed hold of her waist and thrust in even farther. From there, he pumped vigorously in and out as the rocker creaked with the rhythm of their motion.

"Oh god, Clint," she moaned. "Oh my god."

Feeling the sweat break out on his own body, Clint allowed himself to be lost in the moment. The sensation of her body in his hands, his body enveloped by her, and even the sound of her voice were more than enough to drown out everything else around him. Every so often, the rocker would move an unexpected way, which made the sensations all the more exotic and unpredictable.

Clint did allow himself to open his eyes and look down at the sensuous line of Adriana's back. She wriggled slightly back and forth as he moved in and out of her. She was gripping the chair and windowsill so hard that her arms were showing the strain. Even from where he was, Clint could see the outline of the side of her breast as she straightened her back a bit with the approach of her orgasm.

She started to scream, but the sound caught in her throat. Her body stiffened slightly, making her nipple seem to stand out even more in the silhouette that Clint was enjoying.

He could feel the pleasure building up inside of him

until it was finally about to burst. With Adriana tightening around him in the grip of her own climax, Clint held on and drove into her with enough power to push himself over the edge as well as keep Adriana groaning for more.

The force of his orgasm nearly caused Clint's knees to buckle, and when he pulled out of her, he could feel that the blonde was still savoring the presence of him inside of her. She moved back as he did, keeping him between her legs for as long as possible.

Not one to disappoint a lady, Clint reached forward to cup her breasts. The feel of her in his hands combined with her tight ass against his hips was more than enough to keep him rigid and willing, and he was soon slowly pushing inside of her.

"Oh god," she said again. "Oh . . . oh my god! Clint!"

That last exclamation had a whole lot more steam behind it than the others. It struck Clint as more of a scream than anything brought about in the heat of passion. He looked up just in time to see the man's face outside their window, hanging less than an inch from the glass.

THREE

"Holy sh—" was all Clint could get out before the window rattled with another gust of wind that sent the glass knocking against its wooden frame.

No more than half a second went by before the glass was moving again. This time, however, it was being rattled by something much more substantial than the wind. Whoever it was that had been looking into the hotel room was now slamming his fist against the pane and screaming something in a muffled voice.

Clint stumbled backward until the backs of his legs hit the frame of his bed. Without taking his eyes from the window, he snatched up his clothes and hurriedly threw them on. "What the hell? Aren't we on the second floor here?"

If Adriana heard him, she didn't give the slightest clue. She was still staring out the window and trying to climb backwards off the chair.

"Hey!" Seeing that she wasn't paying attention to him, Clint pulled his other arm into his shirt and stepped forward. He could also see that she was about to fall out of the rocker.

Clint wrapped one arm around her waist and lifted her

up off the chair. The man outside had been looking crazy enough, but when he saw Clint pick her up, his face contorted into something from a bad dream. The window rattled once more as the man slammed it with his bare fist. He kept trying to talk as well, but the wind blew away most of his words before they could make it through the window.

After setting her onto her feet, Clint took Adriana by the shoulders and spun her around to face him. "Are you all right?" he asked.

"Y-yes."

"We are on the second floor, aren't we?"

"I . . . I think so."

"Then what the hell is going on? How did that guy get up here?"

"He probably climbed up onto the awning. Milt could always climb almost anything."

Clint started to say something, but stopped short. He took his eyes off the crazy man looking through the window and focused once again on Adriana. "Milt? You mean you know that man?"

She nodded sheepishly and lifted her arms in front of her in a weak attempt to cover herself.

The pounding from outside had stopped, allowing Clint to hear the string of obscenities that were being tossed toward the window. He ignored those for the moment and looked into Adriana's wide eyes. "So who's Milt?"

"He's my . . . husband."

"What!?"

Suddenly, she started shaking her head. "Actually, he used to be my husband. It ended a while ago, but he never got over it. He never got over me, I should say."

When Clint looked back toward the window, he could only see the vague outline of the man outside. The guy's face was contorted with rage, and he was twisting around as though pivoting on his waist.

"Adriana," Milt said. "Whoever that son of a bitch in there is, he's a dead man!" And once that was said, Milt twisted back around and let out a holler which blended in seamlessly with the wind that howled all around him.

Clint had his instincts and experience to thank as he not only spotted the shovel in Milt's hand, but was fast enough to dive for his gun belt before the blade of that shovel shattered the hotel's window.

Glass and cold air rushed into the room, showering over Clint's back as he snatched the Colt from its holster. The window was roughly half the size of the door leading from the hotel room into the hallway. It seemed even bigger than that now that the curtains were blown away by the wind and the only glass that remained was a jagged ring around the edges.

What was left of the window looked like a mouth filled with crystal teeth. And in the middle of that gaping maw was a man crouching down with a shovel clutched in both hands like a club. He peered into the room with wild eyes. Long, dark hair swirled around his head in a thick wind-blown mess. When he shouted, he revealed a crooked set of dirty teeth.

"Adriana, goddammit! How could you do this to me?"

The blonde had already pulled her slip over her head and was tugging it down past her hips. Now that she was covered, she had her hands free to take hold of the first thing she could find. Unfortunately, that first thing was the lantern sitting on a small table next to the bed.

"You're not my husband, Milt!" she shouted. "Not anymore."

Clint hadn't been planning on using the Colt. Not yet, anyway. His main purpose had been to get ahold of the gun so nobody else could use it. And if the maniac outside his window got any ideas, then Clint would at least be ready for it.

FOUR

Looking toward the man who still stood halfway in and halfway out of the room, Clint lowered his gun and said, "Look. There's been a misunderstanding here. I'll just let you two have my room for a bit so you can talk this ov—"

Before Clint could finish his offer, Milt gritted his teeth and lashed out with a burst of strength that surprised even Clint. The shovel in the other man's hands swept in a straight line toward Clint, impacting with a dull clang against fingers and firearm.

Pain spiked through Clint's hand as the cold metal of the shovel's blade slammed against the top of his hand. Although he managed to twist a bit before the shovel hit, to keep from getting his fingers broken, Clint was still forced to drop the Colt.

The gun rattled to the floor as Clint balled up his fists and swung out with the same hand that had just been targeted by Milt's angry blow. As his punch landed upon the other man's chin, Clint figured he might have looked almost as crazy with anger as the guy he'd just hit. Perhaps that was part of the reason that Clint let the Colt drop rather than vent that anger with a bullet.

Milt was still crouching in the window, and when

14

Clint's punch landed on his jaw, it rocked him back out into the night. He would have fallen all the way outside if he hadn't been holding onto that shovel, which still had Clint's blood on it.

As he reeled backward, Milt's arms swung around to try and brace himself. One arm disappeared from Clint's view, but the other made it as far as the top corner of the window before the shovel jammed him in place. Milt hung there suspended, waving his free arm behind him and letting out a crazy shriek.

"I'm gonna fall!" Milt screamed. "For the love of god, Addy, help me!"

Hearing him say that name turned Adriana's frown into a reluctant grin. She looked at the window and then to Clint, pleading with her wide blue eyes while taking a reluctant step toward the broken window. Her feet scraped over some broken glass, which made her stop short. From there, she looked once again at Clint.

Seeing where she was headed before she even said a word, Clint pulled on his boots before he sliced his own feet open. "I thought you said Milt was a good climber."

"He is, but this is a little different. If someone doesn't help him, he could break his neck."

"And by someone, you mean me?"

"I'm not strong enough."

The look in her eyes and the adoring tone in her voice were Adriana's not-too-subtle attempt to win Clint over. He spotted it a hell of a lot better than he'd spotted Milt. Even so, he stomped toward the window and pushed the rocker out of his way.

"Come on, Milt," Clint said as he braced one hand on the wall and used the other to take hold of the shovel handle.

"Get away from me, you bastard!" Milt hollered. "That's the woman I love!"

The pain in Clint's crushed fingers flared up like a

crackle of lightning beneath his skin that raked through every bone in his hand. The sensation caused his jaw to clench and his voice to turn into a haggard snarl. "If you want to do this alone or even break your neck along the way, just let me know."

Milt said something in response to that, but the wind roared around him and swept the breath from out of his lungs. Pulling himself forward, he reached out with his free hand and looked toward Clint.

As much as he wanted to let the other man drop, Clint reached through the broken window and extended his own hand. Behind him, Adriana was getting closer, taking small steps so she could sweep away as much broken glass with her feet as she could. The entire time, she didn't take her eyes off of the man hanging out of the window like so much rumpled, dirty laundry.

"Give me your hand, Milt," Clint said as he strained forward a little more.

The man outside grunted and pulled himself closer. Finally, he was able to twist his upper body and thrust his free hand forward toward Clint. Unfortunately, his reach extended past the hand Clint was offering and went straight on to knock Clint in the eye.

"You bastard! That's the woman I love!"

Clint was so angry at the entire situation by that point, he didn't even feel the impact of Milt's fist. Instead, he simply wondered why he hadn't seen that last punch coming from a mile away. At least it was enough of an excuse to justify him letting go of the crazy, windblown Milt and finding another room somewhere in town.

Let those two fight it out among themselves, Clint thought. They sure as hell deserve each other.

Just as Clint leaned back to get his footing and move away from the window, he realized that the shovel was still in his hand. He'd stepped back a foot or so, but the shovel was still in his hand. Perhaps the knock in the eye had rattled him a little more than he'd thought because Clint found himself lurching forward.

Still gripping the other end of the shovel, Milt had worked it free of the window frame and was using it to drag Clint outside before he had a chance to let it go. In a matter of two seconds, Clint found himself being pulled toward the window, losing his balance and then stumbling to land hanging halfway outside with the wind raging all around him.

The first thing he saw was a pattern of shingles that covered the top of the wooden cover that hung out over the front of the hotel. It didn't look all too sturdy, but it was apparently sturdy enough to hold the weight of the man who was already out there.

Once he'd gotten Clint where he wanted him, Milt jerked the shovel away and raised it over his head. He stared down at Clint as though he barely knew what he was doing. Next, the shovel began swinging downward toward Clint's head.

At that moment, Clint Adams had become even more of a firm believer in bad luck.

FIVE

One thing that Clint had gained from a life on the wild side was an ability to think fast in dangerous situations. It wasn't so much a skill or talent as it was a simple survival tool. If a man got shot at or attacked enough, he could either learn to think fast or die. There were no other options.

Clint's mind snapped into another way of working the instant he saw the way the tide had turned against him. He still didn't want to hurt anyone if possible, but that didn't mean he was about to take a shovel to the skull in the process.

With the blood pumping through his body and his reflexes calling the shots, Clint grabbed hold of the edge of the windowsill and pulled his lower body up until his feet came off the floor. Now that all his weight was on his back against the wooden frame, he lifted his feet up and through the window, holding his boots together as tightly as he could.

If Milt hadn't been winded already, he might have been able to swing a little faster. As it was, he dropped the shovel down, using mostly its own weight. The blunt tool fell a couple feet before it was stopped by the bottom of Clint's boots.

For a second, Milt looked as though he didn't even know what was going on. He still pushed the shovel down with both hands, snarling like an animal with his eyes locked on Clint's face.

Feeling that all the force had been stolen from Milt's swing, Clint tucked his knees in closer to his chest and rolled all the way out onto the awning. Another second was all it took for him to spring to his feet and spin around to look at Milt head-on.

"I don't know about any of this," Clint said. "And I never knew about you. Adriana is a grown woman and she knew what she was doing. If there's more to it than that, I'll step aside."

"More to it? You bet yer ass there's more to it!"

Clint could tell the other man was going to swing even before he'd finished speaking. The muscles in Milt's shoulders were already bunching up, and he'd started inching forward like a snake that was about to strike. Rather than jab with the steel end of the shovel which was already pointed in Clint's direction, Milt hauled the whole thing back over his shoulder and threw out another powerhouse swing.

With plenty of time to get himself ready, Clint waited until the last second before raising his arms up and step-ping back, making himself as narrow a target as possible. The shovel's head cut through the air directly in front of him, with so much force that Clint could feel the air ripple against his midsection.

Now that the shovel was continuing along its path and twisting Milt around with it, Clint lunged forward and snapped out a quick jab to the other man's gut. The punch was mainly to get Milt's attention, as well as to take what little air there still was in the guy's sails.

Milt had been breathing heavily before, and when he

felt Clint's fist poke into his stomach, the awning seemed to tilt slightly beneath his feet. The second jab came right after the first, clouding Milt's vision for a moment and forcing the shovel to slip from one of his hands.

Already, Clint could see that Milt was on his last legs. Like anyone else who was fighting out of pure anger, Milt didn't have nearly enough in his engine to make the long haul. Climbing up to the window and taking his first couple swings had robbed him of most of his steam.

Clint took a second to look around just to make sure he wasn't about to take one hell of a bad step. The awning hung out about six or seven feet from the front of the hotel. Since they were only on the second floor and the awning sloped downward anyway, Clint figured he could easily jump to the street if all else failed. Of course, that wasn't his first choice.

Sticking her head out through the window, Adriana clutched her dress to keep it closed in the howling wind. "Milt! What are you doing out there?" she yelled.

Clint only glanced back at her for a second, still keeping Milt in the corner of his vision. When he looked back, he swore he was looking into the face of another man altogether. This time, Milt was no longer grimacing with rage.

Milt looked mussed by the wind. He looked tired. And he even looked as though he didn't even really know how to answer the question that Adriana had just asked him. For a second, he just stood there, looking at the woman in the window.

"I heard you was in town," Milt said. "Then I heard you was with another man."

Adriana was starting to climb up through the window. Judging by her wobbly movements and uncertain steps, she was probably trying to use the rocking chair as a stepladder. "Where did you hear this?"

"What does it matter where I heard? It's true. You're

here with this other man and . . ." Saying that, Milt turned his attention back to Clint as though he'd almost forgotten he was out there with him.

Stepping back so that the couple could talk, Clint had been more than happy to fade into the background and let those two straighten out whatever they needed to. Now that the talk had turned back to him, Clint could see the anger flaring up in Milt's eyes and filling his body with renewed strength.

"If I can't have ya," Milt said while raising the shovel up over his shoulder, "then this one here sure ain't gonna get ya!"

Now it was Clint who felt tired and worn down. He felt even more so now that he saw his fight with Milt still wasn't over. "Oh, for Christ's sake," Clint snarled as he saw the shovel getting cocked back for yet another swing.

Rather than give Milt another chance to take his head off, Clint pulled his fist back and moved forward until he was less than two feet away from the jealous lover. The rest of the distance between them was closed when Clint drove his fist straight out and into Milt's face, snapping the man's head back with a jarring impact.

First, the shovel dropped from Milt's hand.

Next, his face went blank, as consciousness began to drain out of him.

Finally, Milt staggered forward to where Clint was waiting to catch him in open arms.

But instead of falling the way it appeared he was going, Milt suddenly twisted around and stepped backward. Clint reached out to grab the front of the man's shirt, but Milt's clothes were even shoddier than his sense, and they ripped as soon as Clint got a fistful of them.

Milt teetered for another half second before dropping off the side of the awning and disappearing from Clint's sight.

SIX

"Oh my lord!" Adriana screamed as she hopped down from the rocking chair and ran back into the hotel room.

By that time, Clint was already standing at the edge of the awning, looking down to see where Milt had landed. It wasn't hard to spot the man, since he was the only one standing in front of the hotel, looking up as if he'd just been dropped from the heavens themselves.

Clint couldn't believe his eyes at first. Sure enough, though, Milt was actually standing in the street. As he watched, Clint saw Milt's body start to shake and his knees begin to buckle. In no time at all, Milt let out a cry that would have made a wounded bobcat wince and crumpled over to the ground.

Sitting on the edge of the awning, Clint hung his legs over the side, grabbed on and dropped himself down. Not much after his boots hit the ground, Clint heard the front door to the hotel fly open and Adriana burst outside.

"Are you all right?" she asked while rushing forward.

"It could have been worse, but it's over n—" Clint stopped talking the instant that Adriana ran past him and over to Milt's side, where she knelt down and began fussing over him like a mother hen.

By the look on her face and waver in her voice, Clint might have thought that she was grieving over a dead body rather than some idiot who didn't know how to use a door or stairs. "My sweet baby, are you all right?"

"My legs," Milt grunted. "I think I broke 'em."

Clint walked over to the reunited couple and looked down at them. "What was all that about?" he asked, wondering if he could get Adriana to see the ridiculousness of the whole situation. "Were you following her?"

"I had to see my darlin' girl."

"Through the window?" Clint asked in disbelief. "A second-story window?"

"I had to see you, Addy. I love you!"

Rolling his eyes, Clint muttered, "Jesus Christ."

But Adriana didn't hear him. She didn't seem to be able to look away from Milt's puppy dog eyes or take her hands away from his sweaty brow. "You love me? Really?"

Clint turned away from the pair and walked into the hotel before he was forced to watch them cry. He couldn't decide which annoyed him the most: a man who barged in on him and tried to crush his skull with a shovel, or the woman who found that harder to resist than a bouquet of flowers.

Just as he was about to open the front door, the handle turned and someone stepped through from the other side. It was an elderly man wearing black pants with a white shirt tucked into them. Clint looked down at the black leather bag in the man's hand and took a gamble. "Are you a doctor?" he asked.

"Yes, sir. What's all the commotion? Does that man need help?"

"His legs are broken. When you're done with him, you might want to help the lady."

"What's wrong with her?"

"She needs her head screwed on a little tighter."

From there, Clint stepped aside so the doctor could tend to Milt's broken legs and Adriana could tend to the crazy bastard's broken heart. As far as he was concerned, Clint was just glad to be out of the whole mess with only some battered fingers to show for it.

It had been bad luck to stumble into such a strange situation.

On the other hand, Clint had seen jealousy turn out a whole lot worse. He guessed he could consider it good luck that Adriana had chosen a husband who was as dumb as the trees he was so good at climbing.

Whatever the case might be, Clint was tired and starting to feel as run-down as Milt looked. As soon as he went inside the hotel, he collected his things from his room, turned in his key and went to find another place, where he could get some peace and quiet.

The next morning, Clint woke up to find himself in a room that was about half the size of the one he'd shared with Adriana. The mattress beneath him was not only filled with straw, but the straw was old and flattened after god-only-knew how many bodies had slept on it.

That would teach Clint not to settle for a hotel just because he could see it from the street. Then again, not once throughout the night did some crazed idiot bust through his window. It amazed him sometimes what passed for good news in his life. Rather than dwell on such things, he pulled on his shirt and boots and went to scrounge up some breakfast.

What he found was some runny eggs and bacon that tasted as though it had been cut from an old saddle rather than a hog. Once again, Clint had merely stopped into the first place he could find that might possibly suit his needs. Many times throughout his travels, he'd come across some of the best food he'd ever tasted using that method.

This time, however, he simply got more of the same

bad luck that had been plaguing him over the last few days. Even though the coffee tasted like mud, he'd come to expect it at that point and drank it down anyway. It filled his stomach and got him ready to head out of town, so at least that particular mud had served its purpose.

After saddling Eclipse and climbing onto the Darley Arabian's back, Clint spotted Adriana waiting for the stagecoach at the little depot on the edge of town. Milt was sitting next to her, both legs in splints and a pair of crutches propped up beside him. They both waved and smiled as Clint rode by, as if to thank him for bringing them together.

Seeing that, Clint let out a heavy sigh, snapped the reins and broke Eclipse into a run. If he didn't put that town behind him, whatever the hell its name was, he felt as though he would try to break something else attached to Milt.

Clint had heard certain badmen talk about shooting folks for things as trivial as snoring too loud or interrupting a good meal. Although he didn't agree with such violence, he felt a whole lot closer to understanding it.

SEVEN

All it took was a couple hours of riding in the open country of Montana for Clint to feel his head start to clear and his normal spirits return. The food might have been terrible, but it had filled his belly. The mattress might have been hard and lumpy, but he'd gotten a full night's sleep. And even though Adriana was a foolish woman who was somehow impressed by a crazy man who followed her and stared at her through second-floor windows, she had put one hell of a smile upon Clint's face.

Looking back on the whole thing after a couple hours and several miles had passed, Clint couldn't help but laugh at Milt. The moron might have been a hell of a climber, but his landings left a whole lot to be desired. If he'd had enough brains to pull a trigger without blowing his own damn head off, Milt might have even been dangerous.

Clint still believed in luck, both the good and bad kinds. Most of the time, it was hard not to believe in it. But no matter how much a man believed in luck, Clint knew there was no controlling it. Even the most charmed of rabbit's feet had been bad luck to their original owners. In fact, Clint was one of the few men he knew who gambled and handled a gun but didn't carry some kind of lucky charm.

The only things he relied on were those that would never let him down. Namely, himself, Eclipse and the gun that had been specially modified by his own hand. Far from lucky charms, those things were reliable simply because they were made that way. In the end, that was about all Clint had time to trust.

Once the nameless town was well behind him, all Clint could see was open country that was so beautiful it nearly took his breath away. The air still had the edge of cold, but it wasn't nearly as rambunctious as it had been in town. With so much space to stretch out, the breezes could disperse across the land and roll over it at a much more tranquil pace.

In that way, the air reminded Clint of a herd of buffalo. Slow and steady in the right place, but with enough power to tear a town to bits if it got caught in a confining street.

Letting his mind wander in such a way allowed Clint to pass the next several hours. It took a good portion of that time for him to clear his brain of the strangeness that had taken place the night before. Looking back on it from the proper distance, it all seemed like an odd dream. Even making love to Adriana fit into that frame of mind.

All around him, the trees were coated with leaves in every state of decay. The colors ranged from browns and yellows to brilliant reds and gold. In some places, bare branches stuck out like hundreds of fingers trying to shield the sky from Clint's vision. He left it up to Eclipse to keep to the trail since a good portion of the ground was covered by the thick blanket of autumn.

The Darley Arabian stallion only needed the occasional touch of the reins, and that was mainly to keep him from breaking into a full run. Eclipse was a fine horse, but was still fairly young and had a bit of a wildness that Clint admired. That wildness made Eclipse so reliable because the stallion dedicated all that energy to helping Clint when it was needed.

As a reward for being such a fine horse, Clint let the stallion cover the last several miles of the day galloping to his heart's content. As soon as he knew he'd been given the go-ahead, Eclipse let out a powerful breath which spouted from his nostrils like steam from a piston.

Clint could feel the horse's muscles straining beneath him and had to hold on tight before he was tossed from the saddle from the sheer force of the wind racing over him. For the first time in days, Clint felt like he was the one overpowering those damn winds, and Eclipse cut through them with ease.

Using one hand to hold onto his hat, Clint hunkered down in the saddle and conformed his movements to those of the stallion. For a time, it felt like they were one being, thundering over the land like a force of nature. As the daylight began to fade from the sky, Eclipse's breathing started to get more forced. The stallion was slowing down on his own accord, so Clint pulled back on the reins to bring him to a slower walk.

"All right, boy," he said while reaching out to pat the stallion behind his ears. "Better save some of that fire to get us to a campsite. I'm thinking about something inside that tree line over there."

Clint's eyes were focused on a thick group of trees that were still sporting most of their leaves. As dusk approached, the sky turned the same color as those autumn leaves, blending heaven and earth into one almost seamless display. At that time of year, dusk didn't last too long. That particular sunset, however short, was beautiful enough to last in Clint's memory for a good long time.

It was dark by the time Eclipse finally made it to those trees. Clint dropped down from the saddle as soon as he could, leading the stallion off the trail and to the best clearing he could find. The Darley Arabian seemed grateful when he was tied off, and he huffed a couple tired breaths as Clint kept walking ahead.

There was plenty of firewood to be found, and adding some leaves to the flames gave the fire a smell that reminded Clint of warm nights spent at similar fires from his childhood. No matter what age he was, the smell of autumn was always special to him. Even though it got cold eventually, there was always warmth to be found.

And if he had to wait a bit for that warmth sometimes, it seemed all the more worth it once he did find a fire. It was certainly a different story than being too hot. After all, there wasn't much to be done about the heat of summer; there was only so much a person could do to cool down. Summer was a time to take the heat because there wasn't much other choice. Winter and fall were times for a man to live by his own merits. He could be smart and warm himself up, or he could be foolish and freeze to death.

Despite the brutality of such things, Clint had to admire the simplicity of it all. There were always hard times and different circumstances, but all in all he would prefer to live or die by his own mettle.

For the time being, his only plan was to enjoy his fire, brew up some coffee and fall asleep under the stars. It wasn't long after the sun's rays had disappeared that the stars began to fill the sky above him. He glanced up now and then while he was cooking supper, to take a look at the glittering tapestry overhead.

At that moment, it would have been very easy for Clint to believe that he was the only man on earth. Apart from the constant flow of the wind, there wasn't much else besides the little bit of rustling in the trees around him and the few noises that Eclipse made as he shifted from foot to foot.

Clint sat next to the flickering fire and smiled to himself, picturing that everything else was on another world altogether. More importantly, he seemed to be somewhere that the Milts and Adrianas of the world couldn't find him. At least, for the moment.

And for the moment, that was good enough.

Supper was a simple affair. The beans were hot and the jerky was a chore to chew, but the coffee was just as good as he'd hoped and that made it all worthwhile. Stretching out on the ground with the leaves beneath him and the trees looking down like skeletal guardians, Clint savored the last drop of that coffee and started tracing the lines of all the constellations he could remember.

He managed to work his way through about an eighth of the Greek pantheon before sleep overtook him and the stars became a jumble in his tired brain.

EIGHT

Clint woke up the following morning with more of his body covered by fallen leaves than was covered by his bedroll. After sitting up and dusting himself off, he got the fire going once again to heat up what was left of last night's coffee.

There was just enough in the pot to fill a cup, which was all Clint needed to get himself going. With the crisp air still energizing his body and soul, he decided to eat while on the move and quickly packed up his things. In a matter of minutes, he was on his way. Clint allowed Eclipse to start off slow so the stallion could warm up his muscles a bit, and after half a mile or so, the Darley Arabian was ready to pick up the pace.

Heading west, Clint had the rising sun to his back, which threw a brilliant light over the landscape, a sight that nearly took his breath away. All the colors seemed freshly painted across the trees and ground alike. And just when the sights couldn't get any better, the winds would pick up and swirl the leaves about, making it seem as though a work of art had just been brought to life before his very eyes.

Even before noon, Clint would have had a hard time

remembering who Milt and Adriana were. Those two and all the aggravation they represented had been pushed to the back of his mind, hopefully forever. There was a whole world in front of him to think about and Clint wasn't about to let himself get so distracted from it.

The trail he'd been following took him through a thin patch of trees before emptying out onto a vast stretch of open land. As soon as he broke through, something caught his eye in the distance. He might not have seen it at all if not for the bit of motion that moved differently than everything else around.

With the winds stirring everything up and tossing it about like a bored child swatting its toys, Clint had gotten to the point where none of the movements seemed random at all. He'd been watching the path of the wind until it seemed to be a living, breathing thing sharing his space. The motion he saw in the distance didn't fit into that pattern. In fact, it was going completely against the grain.

For a minute or so, Clint didn't think too much of it. After all, he didn't seriously think he was attuned to the breeze so much that he could predict what it was going to do next. But after that motion had caught his eye, he kept his gaze leveled in that direction and watched with growing interest.

The motion started off as a speck in the distance that seemed to be moving contrary to all the other specks.

After concentrating on it a few more minutes, Clint realized that he'd actually spotted another rider headed in his direction. The horse in the distance had been tough to spot simply because of the trees and the multitude of other colors in the background. Clint knew the rider must be headed in his direction because otherwise the horse would have already been swallowed up by those trees.

As soon as he'd identified what it was, Clint got Eclipse moving a little faster. The Darley Arabian had no trouble accommodating the request and surged forward with a burst of energy.

Most travelers new to the vast spaces of the West were fooled by the wide-open landscapes. A mountain range could look close enough to touch, but never get any closer after days of riding. Clint had covered enough ground to not be tricked by such things and to use other means to judge how far away the other rider truly was.

In fact, since the second horse seemed to be moving as well, it made the task even easier. Rather than look at his destination, Clint focused on how far the other horse seemed to go in a certain amount of time. That, combined with a guess of how fast the horse might be going got him thinking that he would meet the other rider in less than half an hour. It wasn't an ironclad figure, but it was the best he could do for the moment.

Clint didn't have any good reason to concern himself at all with that other horse. After he'd convinced himself that it was indeed another rider, he steered himself in that direction just to give him some point to call a target. He always enjoyed riding after something for the sake of riding after it, and he was familiar enough with the country to know that he'd be able to find a town before his situation could get too grim.

Even if he passed that second horse in a matter of seconds, that wasn't the point. He was simply picking a dot on the horizon and setting that as his new course. It wasn't any more complicated than that.

The scenery in front of him did get a little more interesting in the next couple minutes, however. Instead of the single rider on the trail ahead, he started to pick out other shapes emerging from the tree line in the distance. Since he'd covered some ground, Clint was better able to see the figures, and now he also knew what to look for.

As far as he could tell, there were at least four other horses coming up behind the first rider he'd spotted. It was still a little hard to tell since those others were apparently still within the trees after all. It was only thanks to the sun shining from over Clint's shoulder that he was able to spot them before they emerged.

Something in the pit of Clint's stomach shifted and it wasn't that terrible breakfast he'd had back in the previous town. He couldn't quite put his finger on it, but that feeling made him touch his heels to Eclipse's sides, causing the stallion to add a little more steam to his strides.

It seemed as though the rider closest to Clint had gotten that same burr under his saddle, since that horse was getting closer a lot faster than Clint had anticipated. The two would probably meet in about five more minutes. Possibly less if the other rider dug his spurs in and snapped his reins.

The pounding of the other horse's hooves had already reached Clint's ears and was growing louder by the second. Some of that noise was probably left over from several minutes ago and had only then just reached him, like slow ripples moving over a still pond. But the noises Clint heard as the horse came into clearer view were most definitely fresh.

Not only was there the thunder of the animal's charge, but a voice began creeping into Clint's ears as well. Although he couldn't make out what the man was saying, Clint could tell it was something urgent. That feeling came to a boil as the first gunshot cracked through the air.

NINE

It didn't take much coaxing to bring Eclipse up to full speed. As soon as he heard the shooting start, all Clint had to do was snap the reins and the Darley Arabian damn near seemed to take flight. He covered the distance between Clint and the other rider in hardly any time at all. Part of that was also due to the fact that the other man had been driving his horse almost into the ground.

As the distance closed, Clint could make out a few details concerning that other rider. He appeared to be a thin fellow and was no stranger to a saddle. He moved on top of that horse as though he knew what the animal was thinking. Clint guessed him to be around average height, but it was still hard to say, since the other man was keeping his head low.

The rider's hat had blown off and was hanging around his neck by a cord, revealing a head of dark, close-cropped hair. Clint could also make out the man's beard since it was the same coal black as the stubble atop his head.

The pair drew close so quickly that it seemed they might collide. Like the mountains that Clint had been thinking about earlier, the other man didn't appear to get within shouting distance until they were about to butt heads. Both riders knew what they were doing well enough to compensate for the minor optical illusion.

Clint pointed to his right and then steered Eclipse in that direction. Sure enough, the other rider followed suit and came up alongside once both men were pointed north.

More shots broke through the air, but whoever was pulling their triggers was too far away to hit either Clint or the man riding next to him. It was possible that those others were hunters, but even the most daring of gamblers wouldn't put much on those odds.

"What's the hurry?" Clint shouted to the other rider.

Taking one quick look to his left, the second man flicked his reins to keep up with Eclipse's powerful strides. "I got a bit of a bandit problem. They ambushed me and my partner a few miles west of here."

"Partner? Where's he?"

"I couldn't tell you. We split up and are supposed to meet up again in a few hours. I only hope he made it away from those bastards without getting shot full of holes."

"How many robbers?"

"There were seven or eight to start with." The man looked back toward the trees again, trying to focus on the shapes that were just then emerging from their limited cover. "Looks like some of them took off after my partner." Turning to Clint, he added, "Or they might be circling around to cut me off."

Clint looked back toward the trees as well. As far as he could tell, there were only four or five of the others still in pursuit. Most of the shapes were easier to see now that they were out of the trees, but that didn't mean that all of them were present and accounted for.

"This is pretty open country," Clint called out. Now that they'd gotten used to the sound of both horses' combined footfalls, they could hear each other without having to scream every word. "Do you know of anyplace where you could get to that might be a safe hiding spot?"

"I was headed for a cave in a patch of woods about half a mile northeast of here. If I could get a little ways ahead, I might be able to make it there."

"How much of a lead do you need?"

The man thought about it for a second or two and then glanced back at the riders coming up from behind. "All I need is to get into some better cover. After that . . . a minute or two would go a long ways in letting me find a place to hole up."

"I'll see what I can do," Clint said. "What about your partner? Is he headed for that same cave?"

"Yeah."

"What's his name?"

"Alex Wright. He's a big fella with blond hair. Looks like a Dutchman."

"I'll keep an eye out for him." The shots had tapered off a bit now that the group of riders in the distance had gotten their sights set on their target. Clint took another look at them and scanned the area around him. "Head straight for that ridge," he said, pointing to a hill that rose sharply less than an eighth of a mile directly ahead of them. "Go for cover and then swing around toward your cave. I'll see if I can get them running in the other direction."

"Much obliged, stranger."

"Call me Clint and don't thank me yet. I'll want to talk to you when we get clear of this, and besides, we're a long way from that anyhow." Clint drew his Colt and held it pointing toward the sky. "Break off on the count of three. I'm gonna shoot at you, but that's only for show. Understand?"

"I understand. You sure you're good enough to miss me at this distance?"

"There's one good way to find out. One . . . two . . . three!"

The other man turned sharply away from Clint right on cue. He dug his heels into the sides of his horse and shouted for the animal to pour on every bit of strength he had.

Clint pulled back on Eclipse's reins to slow the stallion down. He even wavered in the saddle and steered the Darley Arabian in a few awkward angles before sighting down the barrel of his gun. By the time he took his first shot, Clint had to pull his hand up and to the side to keep from hitting the other man. The second shot came another second or two later, and by the time he took his third, the other man was out of the pistol's range.

Swearing at the top of his lungs, Clint kept his pistol in hand and brought Eclipse around to face the other oncoming riders. He knew the other men had seen the display and had probably even heard his shouted curses. Now the only thing left was to see how they would react.

TEN

It wasn't that Clint thought the first man was lying. In fact, he saw the fear in that one's eyes plain as day and knew he was truly running for his life. But Clint had learned long ago to trust his instincts, and those instincts told him that there was more to what the man was saying than what he'd decided to tell.

Something in Clint's gut told him those other men were dangerous, but they would most likely do something else besides try to hold him up once he got to them. Most bandits weren't desperate enough to jump two men traveling alone, especially when there were plenty of bigger fish to hook and hardly anyone around to see them fishing.

And even if they did decide to take out those two for whatever reason, it was even more strange to Clint that those bandits would go to so much trouble to chase them down, shooting at them and trying to catch them for a mile or so, perhaps. But even now Clint could feel the determination surging through that entire group. They were after something more than some money or valuables.

They were after blood.

He could see that hunger in their eyes even before he could really see their eyes. It was something that pulsed

39

from them like heat from the barrel of a gun. You might not have been able to see the heat that spewed from that muzzle. You might not even be able to hear the shot, but you could most definitely feel it. And if you stood in its way, the heat would burn you down.

The riders were coming up to Clint in a rush. They swarmed around him like giant insects and hardly even slowed down before sweeping him up along with them. Of course, it helped that Clint had been planning on being swept away from the moment he'd fired that first shot over the other man's head.

There were five of them in all. Four of those thundered on after giving Clint no more than a passing glance. The last of them slowed his horse so quickly that the animal reared up and pumped its front legs into the air before dropping down again.

Sitting on top of that horse was a bulky man who appeared to be in his mid to late fifties. He wore a suede leather jacket that looked as though it had been stitched together from several freshly skinned bulls. Thick, silvery gray hair streamed down to his shoulders from beneath a large Stetson hat, sporting a band decorated with red and brown beads. A bushy gray mustache covered his top lip, giving him the look of a trapper or mountain man.

Clint took his cue from that man and brought Eclipse up alongside of him. Neither horse came to a stop, but merely followed the others at a pace which made it easier for the riders to talk to one another.

"And who the hell are you?" the man asked while giving Clint a thorough once-over.

"Funny. I was about to ask you the same question."

"I'm after that man you were talking to a moment ago."

"Talking to?" Clint said as both he and the other man started following in the others' wake. "I was letting my gun here do most of my talking for me."

"Yeah, I saw that. That's why I even bothered stopping

to say anything to you at all. You want a piece of that asshole, too?"

"I wouldn't mind. Especially since he tried to get my horse right out from under me just because I bothered to ask what the hell was going on."

"Is that a fact?"

"Sure is. By the way, what the hell is going on here?"

The silver-haired man smirked without a trace of humor and looked ahead toward the rest of the riders. "I'd be happy to tell you the story once we get ahold of that skunk. If you want to help, we'd be happy to have you. If not, then stay back here where it's safe."

Not waiting for a reply, the older man snapped his reins and sent his horse into a run. The animal was in fine condition. So much so that Clint figured it even had a good chance of catching up with the other four.

Clint had managed to hold the older man back, but the other four were still riding ahead. He swore under his breath and touched his heels to Eclipse's sides. That was all the Darley Arabian had to feel before building up his speed until the breath was churning from his lungs.

Fortunately, the silver-haired man seemed to be the leader of the group. That much was obvious since the remaining four riders hadn't been as eager to move too far ahead of him. Both the older man and Clint were able to catch up to the others. Only after the silver-haired man pulled into the lead did the entire group pick up its pace once again.

That was somewhat in Clint's favor, but he still needed to keep the group back a bit more if the first man was going to make it to that cave he'd talked about. Part of Clint didn't even believe there was a cave. What he did believe was the fact that those five men were dead set on a kill once they got ahold of their target.

Murder didn't set well in Clint's gut. Neither did an unfair fight. At the very least, he aimed to find out what had started this chase. In order to do that, however, he was going to have to find out how the chase ended.

Eclipse was starting to breathe heavier, but he still overtook the other five horses with some degree of ease. Before he pulled up next to the silver-haired man again, Clint scanned ahead to see how far ahead the rabbit was from the hounds.

That first rider was actually doing pretty well for himself. He hadn't made it to the ridge yet, but he would be there in under a minute or so. Clint could still feel the hunger for blood hanging in the air over the other riders like a foul-smelling cloud that followed their every move. For that reason, he rode to the head of the pack until he was next to the older man in the lead.

Several of the others tried to stop him, but their horses simply weren't up to the task of chasing down a contender like Eclipse.

"Damn!" snarled the silver-haired man. "That bastard's about to get around that ridge."

"Good thing I came along then," Clint said. "Because I know where he's headed."

The older man looked over and nodded as a smile grew across his face. "Welcome aboard, son. You just officially joined this posse."

ELEVEN

The riders sure didn't seem like lawmen. Keeping toward the head of the pack, Clint kept from reacting one way or another to what the silver-haired man had said. It might have been anything from fact to just an expression. The group might have been a real posse or not. Clint didn't see any badges, but that didn't mean there weren't any to be found.

For the time being, he decided to play out his hand and see what happened.

They were quickly approaching the ridge where Clint had told the first man to go. Even though he wasn't completely sure how far to trust any of the men, Clint was positive that first rider didn't want to get caught by the ones following him. For that reason alone, he knew it would be a safe bet to assume the plan was still going on as scheduled.

After coming around the bend where the ground swelled up into a rise, the silver-haired man held up one hand, signaling for everyone else to stop. "All right, then," he said, looking over to Clint. "Since we lost sight of him, why don't you tell us what you know?"

"He asked me if I'd seen some other fella that was

supposed to be over that way," Clint answered, nodding in the opposite direction from where the first man was supposed to be headed. "I told him I saw him just so he'd move on and that seemed to be the way he was going."

"Another fella, huh?"

"That's what he said."

"You men check it out." And with a nod in the direction Clint had pointed, the silver-haired man sent three of the others on their way. "The rest of you come with me. Including you."

Clint nodded. "You think he might be trying to get us turned around?"

"Could be."

"Then maybe I should go off with those other men and check out the only path I really know about."

"No offense, mister, but I don't even know your name. I'd rather keep you where I can see you."

"The name's Clint Adams."

The silver-haired man reacted fairly close to what Clint had been expecting. There was a moment of disbelief and then the slow, careful glance as his eyes dropped immediately to the gun in Clint's hand. "I've heard of you. Just so long as you really are who you say you are."

"With the things you've probably heard about me, you must know there wouldn't be many men foolish enough to impersonate me once the shooting had already started."

The silver-haired man smirked and shrugged. "Maybe. I'm Dave Fischer. Like I said, I don't mean any offense, but I've already got enough worries without me taking on some new help in the middle of it all. Even if you said you was Wyatt Earp, I'd ask you to stick close for the moment. I'm sure you understand."

"No problem at all." Clint had barely even been paying attention to the conversation. Instead, he'd been more concerned with ticking off the seconds, balancing how much more time he could waste before it started to look suspicious. So far, he was satisfied that he'd given the first rider a decent head start without making it obvious that that was what he was doing.

"Come on," Fischer said. "Let's check out this way just to be sure and then we'll meet up with my men."

"And what if they find him first?"

"Then I'm sure we'll hear the shots."

Obviously through with talking, Fischer snapped his reins and sent his ash-colored horse galloping along the ridge. Clint noticed that Fischer's remaining man stayed behind to follow in Clint's path. So far, that man hadn't given so much as a nod to the party's newest member. But Clint could feel that one's gaze like sunlight focused through a magnifying glass at a point between his shoulders.

Fischer took off at a decent pace and Clint followed behind him. The silver-haired man was looking to and fro for any trace of his prey, and Clint followed suit. It wasn't hard to blend in at that point because Clint truly was trying to pick up a hint as to where the first rider had gone.

There weren't a whole lot of places to hide once the so-called posse had gotten around the rise. The trail was wide enough for two horses to walk side by side, and it was lined on one side by the incline of earth and rock. On the other side was a patch of trees which didn't thicken too much until about twenty paces off the beaten path.

If he was looking for the other man on his own, Clint would have sat still for a moment so he could listen at everything around him. At that time of year more than any other, it was a benefit to be tracking someone around so many trees.

Although the other two men weren't making it any easier for him to hear, Clint also knew that they were having just as difficult a time, and that was the entire point. Fischer had his gun up and ready as though he expected to put a bullet into the first living thing that caught his eye. Still following the older man's lead, the rider behind Clint got his pistol ready. The metallic snap of the hammer being cocked back rattled through Clint's ears.

They were headed along the rise, and it wouldn't take much time before they came around to the other side. The rise itself didn't go for more than fifty yards or so before it tapered off and sank back down into level ground. Fischer was just over halfway to the end when he motioned for the others to stop.

"Hold it," the silver-haired man said. "Did you two hear that?"

Clint had heard the snap of dry leaves being crushed and was just searching out the source of the sound. He found it almost as soon as Fischer had finished asking his question. Although he was hidden pretty well considering what he had to work with, the first rider could just be seen in the distance among a thick clump of trees.

Pointing to a spot away from the path, Clint said, "I see him."

TWELVE

Both Fischer and the man behind Clint looked to where he was pointing and immediately spotted the shape huddled there. The rise and the trees were providing some shadows, the main thing that could keep anything out of plain sight. Now that Clint had pointed it out, however, both the others had no trouble knowing where to ride.

The horses let out a powerful breath as they turned and headed toward the shape huddled in the trees. Clint waited a second, until the man who'd stayed behind him thundered past, too wrapped up in the thrill of the chase to worry about keeping so close an eye on him any longer. Once he was certain the other two were occupied for the moment, he steered Eclipse away from the rest and took off full speed down the path.

After covering about twenty feet, Clint turned Eclipse into the trees until he got a clear view of the figure that had truly caught his attention among the trees. The first rider was huddled down behind a thick, rotting tree trunk and his horse was laying on the ground not too far behind him. In fact, the man had done a good job of keeping low, and the only reason Clint had found him first was because he knew what to look for and where to point his eyes.

Even though the horse was laying down, it was obviously a long way from being rested. In fact, Clint thought the poor animal might have a hard time getting back up to its feet. The rider didn't look in much better shape, and it was all he could do to keep his ragged breaths from making too much noise.

Clint rode Eclipse a little closer to where the man was hiding and looked down at him. "You keep heading for that cave," he said. "I'll meet up with you there tonight, and if you're not there to meet me, I'll tell these men exactly where you were hiding, and I'm sure they can pick up your tracks from there. And if they can't, I'll help them."

The man nodded weakly and looked more than a little taken aback by Clint's tone. "I'll be there. I don't have much other place to go."

"You'd better be there." And with that, Clint turned Eclipse away and headed back to meet up with Fischer and the others.

The longer he thought about what he might have gotten himself into, the more opportunities he saw for it all to go wrong. As always, he'd let his instincts guide him into another sticky situation where someone's life was in danger. Unfortunately, those situations also put his own life in danger. He knew that only too well.

Clint's detour and conversation with the man in hiding had taken less than a minute. Even so, he felt an uneasy sensation in his belly that told him it had been a minute too much and he would most certainly be missed. Fischer had taken the bait Clint dangled in front of him quickly enough, but he doubted he could get away with such a trick again. But if things went well enough, Clint wouldn't have to rely on such tactics again.

As soon as Clint had ridden away to meet up with Fischer, he could hear movement as the first man started heading in the other direction. Clint pulled Eclipse hard

to the left and then back again so that once Fischer or his
other helper spotted him again, Clint would pull their eyes
away from the man trying to get away.

He wasn't completely sure what was what, but until
Clint saw a badge or some other evidence that Fischer
was right in hunting another man down, he wanted to keep
everyone on both sides of this alive. Clint had seen too
many vigilante mobs, and the very notion of a lynching
left a rotten taste in his mouth.

After getting a good look at both that first rider and his
horse, Clint was certain neither one of them would get
too much farther without some rest. Even if the man decided to take off on his own, Clint had already figured
the size of the area he'd have to search to track him down.

If that first rider was truly being hunted for no good
reason, Clint wasn't about to stand by and let someone
put a bullet through his skull. If that man was in the
wrong, Clint would find him and bring him in himself.
Either way, he figured his part in the matter would take
no more than a day.

With that somewhat comforting thought in mind, Clint
met up with Fischer and the man who'd been at his side.
Both of the others looked even more suspicious of Clint
than when they'd first laid eyes on him.

"Where did you get off to?" Fischer asked.

"I thought I heard someone else moving over there,"
Clint replied, hooking his thumb in the general direction
from which he'd come. "Did you find him?"

Fischer's eyes narrowed and he was obviously studying
every last detail in Clint's face. Clint recognized that kind
of scrutiny, but he was usually the one glaring like that.

The silver-haired man paused for a second, until he'd
seen enough, and then said, "Nah. That was just some
deer you spotted. What about you?"

Clint shook his head. "More deer. As soon as I saw
what it was I came back around to meet you."

"I guess we might as well meet up with the rest of the boys," Fischer said, more to the other man than Clint. "If that son of a bitch was anywhere around here he would have taken off by now. Let's just hope them others had better luck than we did."

"That wouldn't be too hard," the other man said, disproving Clint's theory that the man was a mute. "Since we didn't have any luck at all. Not once this one showed up."

Rather than say anything right away, Fischer turned to Clint to see how he would react to hearing those words. The look in the older man's eyes was a mixture of curiosity and amusement. He seemed to be genuinely looking forward to what might happen.

Despite the control he had over himself, Clint felt his emotions spike when he heard the smugness in the other man's voice, and saw the condescending look on his face. Even so, Clint was too good a poker player to let such simple things show through with so little provocation.

"Hey, I tried," Clint said simply. "If you don't want my help, then I'll be on my way."

Fischer rode forward and waved away the other man's comments. "Nonsense, Adams. Come along with us. My ranch is a few miles from here, and it's the only place for a day's ride in any direction. The least I can do for trying to help me is give you a meal and a cot for the night. What do you say?"

"I'd be much obliged, Mr. Fischer."

"Good. Then that means I can count on you for the rest of the day?"

Even though he felt as if he'd just been roped in like a calf in a rodeo, Clint nodded and said, "Sure. Why not?"

THIRTEEN

Fischer took his time riding to meet up with the rest of his men. He was still searching the area for any trace of his quarry, and the other man with him was still watching Clint like a hawk. As long as one of those men was watching him, Clint figured he didn't have to worry about distracting him from finding who they were really after. All that remained was to position himself like a human blind so that he blocked Fischer's view of the first rider's escape as much as possible.

The more time he spent with Dave Fischer, the more Clint figured he was doing the right thing in helping that solitary rider. So far, he was fairly convinced that Fischer wasn't a bandit, but he had yet to see any sign of a badge either. In fact, Clint still didn't really know what was on Fischer's mind at all.

Since the shortest distance between two points was still a straight line, Clint decided to get his answer the old-fashioned way. Flicking the reins, he took Eclipse on that straight line which ended at Fischer's side. "So what's got you so fired up to find this man anyway?" Clint asked.

Fischer smiled. The gesture curled the edges of his brushy mustache like a fat, hairy caterpillar that had been shriveled in the sun. "Funny you'd ask. Especially since you were shooting at him a couple seconds after meeting him yourself."

"He wanted to steal my horse. I don't have too big a problem shooting any man who'd try something like that." This time, Clint didn't have to put any effort at all into making his voice sound steely and cold. It always helped to keep a story as close to the truth as possible.

"Well, he not only stole that horse he was riding from me, but he killed three of my men as well. And that was only when he was trying to get away from my ranch after molesting my daughter."

"Are you serious?"

"Take a look, Adams," Fischer said while turning to stare directly into Clint's eyes. "Does it look like I'm joking?"

Clint's first impulse was to take Fischer at his word. Then again, the silver-haired man had looked dead serious from the first moment he'd introduced himself, and now was no exception. "Well, if he tried to take my horse, he must have run that one he stole down to the bone. He probably can't get too far."

"That's what I've been thinking. But that doesn't mean he won't try."

"You could always tell the law about this."

Fischer looked over at Clint as though he'd just been told to try eating his hat. "Tell the law? There's no need to bring the law in on this. Besides, there ain't no law close enough to tell anyway."

At least that cleared up one thing inside Clint's mind. The comment that had been made about a posse had just been talk after all. Not that it was any big revelation. Fischer and his men didn't have the feel of lawmen about them. Well, not the type of lawmen that could be trusted, anyway.

"The law's got to be told sooner or later, don't they?"

Clint asked, trying to keep his voice as innocent as possible.

"They do? Why's that?"

"Well, what do you plan on doing to this man if you find him?"

"Oh, we'll find him, all right. Don't you worry about that."

"All right then. When you find him, what are you planning to do with him?"

Once again, Fischer glanced over to look directly in Clint's eyes. All that needed to be said was said without a word passing from his lips. His eyes said it all. They glinted like two iron marbles lodged in his skull. Whatever light there was inside of them seemed more like an illusion. They were just too cold to convey anything but bad intentions.

"When we find him," Fischer said, "I'm going to make him sorry he ever even met my daughter. Then, after a few days of that have gone by, I'll make him sorry he was ever even born."

"That's usually a job for a judge and jury isn't it?"

For a second or two, Fischer looked as though he couldn't believe the words that had just flown from Clint's mouth. Once again, he seemed to be waiting for the punch line of a bad joke, and when it didn't come, he started laughing anyway.

"A judge and jury." Turning around so he could look past Clint at the man who'd taken it upon himself to act as Clint's shadow, Fischer said, "Did you hear that, Jonah? Mr. Adams here is asking about a judge and jury."

Up until that moment, Clint had merely considered the man following him as an obstacle that he needed to work around. Now that he'd done what he could for the moment to keep that first rider alive, Clint allowed himself to take a better look at the man riding behind him.

It wasn't a surprise that Clint had been able to look

past, around and damn near through Jonah in the first place. He was a big guy and took up a lot of space, but that was about it. His bulky, muscular body filled out a set of unremarkable clothes and his doughy face had about as much inner spark as a melon with horse hair glued to it.

Jonah laughed at Fischer's joke a little too hard and tried to appear menacing when he caught Clint staring at him. Although his eyes reflected a taint of meanness, it reminded Clint of something he might see in the face of a dog.

No, maybe an ox. Clint thought a dog was probably smarter than an ox.

"I thought you were smarter than that, Mr. Adams," Fischer said, once it was obvious that Jonah wasn't about to add anything to the conversation. "From what I've heard, you've been around long enough to know that the law can't be everywhere."

"That's true."

"So, in that case, a man's got to enforce the law himself."

"Or just make it up as he goes."

There was a tense silence as soon as Clint said that. Fischer seemed as though he was trying to decide between two courses of action, and Clint had a good idea what those choices were.

"Tell you what, Adams," Fischer said finally. "Why don't you help me if you know so much? Let me show you what you're dealing with and then you can tell me what needs to be done about it."

FOURTEEN

Fischer's group of men hadn't searched the entire area by a long shot. However, because they could see so much through the open spaces and bare branches of the surrounding trees, it was obvious that if they were going to find anyone they would have done it by now. Their target was long gone. They knew it. And not one of them was happy about it.

Despite the fact that his own anger made his features tense and his eyes appear even more steely than usual, Fischer did a good job of keeping his rage to himself. He rounded up his men quickly, telling them just what they needed to know without going into details. He made sure to keep Clint close by and expressed his inclination toward him to his men with subtle looks and slight gestures.

Clint might not have even noticed the signals Fischer was passing, but the reactions from the other men were unmistakable. One second they would be looking at him with curiosity or mistrust and the next they would be studying his every move. All it had taken was a nod from their boss or a slight wave of his hand for the change to happen. Once it did, though, that change was unmistakable.

Clint pretended not to notice those things, however. Doing so would have only been tipping his hand, and that was a mistake that only players new to the game would make. Clint had played this game only too many times. Although it was never the same game twice, the rules were simple and always the same:

Find out what the other players want and why.

Find out if they are friend or foe.

And, most importantly: Always know more about the other person than they know about you.

It was never easy to do, but if Clint could keep ahead on all those fronts, he stood a chance of winning this game. The rules were simple, but the prize was great.

Life or death.

It was plain to see that Fischer was playing for the highest of stakes. As long as there was the slightest chance that someone else might be sitting at the table not of his own free will, Clint felt an obligation to see that that man wasn't robbed of his greatest prize.

Men like Fischer and plenty of others liked to talk about their ideas of law and order, justice and punishment. The way Clint saw it, all those things boiled down to a simple code. A man had to help those that needed to be helped.

That was the only law.

If everyone stuck to that one simple rule, Clint figured the world would be a whole lot better off.

So far, his gut was telling him that the first rider he'd met was a hair's length away from getting his neck stretched at the end of a short rope. And after riding with him for a good part of the day, Dave Fischer wasn't telling him anything different.

In fact, once he'd called off the search near the rise, Fischer hadn't really told Clint much of anything. From that point on, he'd ridden to the head of the group and was leading them back along the same direction from which they'd first appeared.

All of the men had received their silent orders and were carrying them out to the letter. Clint could feel every one of their eyes on him as though he was the only bird at a turkey shoot. But he didn't let the bull's-eye on his back dampen his spirits. Instead, he kept his expression neutral and his eyes fixed straight ahead.

It was best to let men like those think they had the upper hand. That was when they were bound to get cocky, and once that happened, they were sure to make mistakes. For that reason alone, Clint suffered through all the bad looks and unspoken threats that were tossed his way. He'd seen a whole lot worse from men that were a whole lot meaner.

Now that they were going back over their own tracks, Fischer's group no longer seemed to be in any hurry. They rode at a decent pace, but weren't straining their horses any more than they already had. Clint could feel the relief coming from every one of the animals, as though he could understand what they were thinking.

All of the animals had their heads down and their hooves dragging. They'd been ridden hard for quite a while and it showed. In fact, Clint was starting to wonder just how far they'd gone before breaking through the trees where he'd first spotted them. If it was much farther, he might have to come up with a way to separate from the group after all.

Before Clint could get too anxious, Fischer raised his hand and brought the entire group to a stop. "There," the silver-haired man said. "You wanted to know what this is all about. Take a look for yourself."

Clint had ridden up to look at what Fischer was referring to when something hit him like a slap in the face. It was the smell of blood, and it damn near dropped him from the saddle.

FIFTEEN

It took a moment or two for the sight to truly sink into Clint's eyes. Actually, his eyes were taking in more than enough. It was his brain that needed some time to sift through all the things he was seeing. The coppery stench of blood hung in the air like smoke, sticking to his clothes just as much as it stuck to the inside of his nostrils and the back of his throat.

He could feel his stomach starting to clench and the tickle of a gag reflex kicking in. Clint pulled the bandanna around his neck up so it could cover his nose. That wasn't enough to cut the smell out entirely, but it allowed him to take a few steadying breaths without gagging on them.

The scene in front of him was something straight out of a nightmare. Clint was no stranger to blood and death, but that didn't mean he was on friendly terms with either one. As he climbed down from his saddle, Clint kept one hand holding the bandanna over his mouth and nose. He didn't lower the strip of cloth until it too began to stink of death.

The area directly in front of Clint was a clearing that was roughly circular and no more than twenty feet across. At the farthest edge was a flatbed wagon that was the size of something used by farmers when they went into town for supplies. When it was in one piece, it was probably only about six or seven feet long and as wide as a coffin. Now the wagon was laying on one side and busted nearly in half. Two of the wheels were jammed against the earth. The rough winds blew through the trees fast enough to turn the other two wheels in slow, squeaky circles.

By the looks of it, the cart had been broken apart against a tree or rock which would have overturned it. From there, it must have been torn apart by something else. Human hands were Clint's first guess, but a cannon would have done almost as much damage. There were ripped burlap sacks and busted crates scattered around the wreck, which must have been stacked in the cart at one time.

Clint had been paying so much attention to the heap of broken wood as a way to take his mind off the other kind of wreckage strewn about. Steeling himself with a deep breath, he looked down at the bodies littering the earth.

There were three that he could see right away. Two men and one woman, judging by the way they were dressed. He had to go by that primarily because their skin was wrapped around their bones like sheets of rotten jerky. The dirt around each corpse was soaked through with blood and worse. The ground was moist beneath Clint's feet.

The rest of the men had fanned out around the perimeter of the small clearing, most of them turning their faces away or even starting to back away completely. Fischer sat in his place with his hands folded over the saddle horn. He looked down at the grisly scene as though he needed to burn it into his eyes.

Clint looked around at the clearing, focusing on the trees and leaves scattered about. Forcing himself to blunt his reaction to the carnage, he thought of specific things to look for. At least that pushed back his urge to wretch. "Was there a fire?" he asked.

The question didn't seem right because although the cart itself looked as though it might have been blackened in certain parts, the trees and ground didn't look as though they'd been touched by flame. At that time of year, a fire might have burned down every tree in sight.

Fischer took a while to respond. He seemed to be transfixed by the gruesome spectacle splayed out before him. "Yeah, there was a fire. This whole place reeked of kerosene when I found it. That stench was what brought me here in the first place."

Gritting his teeth, Clint stepped closer to the nearest body and squatted down beside it. When he got within a couple feet of the corpse, he could smell the kerosene as well. If it hadn't been for the winds blowing in the wrong direction, he would have picked up on it much sooner.

He tilted his head and looked a little closer. All the bodies were facedown, and when he could see the closest one a little better, he noticed the skin was charred and burnt, sticking to the bones like greasy tarp. Clint guessed the corpse was a male, but that was only due to the boots and what might have been jeans that had been melted onto the body. Now that he was closer, the fire damage was unmistakable. The only reason there had been any question at all was that he hadn't looked so carefully.

Of course, being a human being, it wasn't Clint's first impulse to make guesses about what might have happened during a tragedy like this. That kind of work was left more to the monsters of the world.

The rest of the bodies weren't in much better condition. The wind had died down just enough for the stink of kerosene to rise up from the earth and remind everyone it was still there. Clint walked around the site just to take it all in. As he did, his mind raced with a way to figure out what could have caused such a thing.

"Now do you see?" Fischer asked. "I'm going to have nightmares about this for the rest of my life. Now do you see why I need to get my hands on the son of a bitch that did this?"

"You mentioned something happened to your daughter," Clint said as tactfully as he could manage under the circumstances. "Is she . . . ?"

"No. She's not anywhere near here. She's back at my home under guard and behind as many doors as I could lock."

"Who were these people?"

Once again, Fischer's eyes drifted toward the bodies. Mainly, he seemed to be looking at the woman laying in the bed of dirt and leaves on the opposite side of the cart from Clint. "Those men were some of my finest workers. They weren't doing anything but taking some things to a trading post not too far from where I live."

"Could they have been after the cargo?"

"Maybe at first. But they weren't really carrying anything too valuable. Just some surplus feed and blankets. My daughter and sister make the blankets so well that they fetch a damn good price, but I don't know any thieves that would be after such things. My sister did say she met some shady characters at the trading post a few weeks ago."

"What about your sister?" Clint asked. "Might she know anything useful?"

"I'd say you could ask her, but that's her laying right over there."

Clint looked over to where Fischer was staring. The wind picked up and bristled against the flaps of charred material stuck to that corpse's dress.

SIXTEEN

Just about every part of Clint's mind and soul wanted to get as far away from that clearing as possible. The only part that kept him there was the part that got him into the most trouble throughout his entire life. It was the same part that caused him to go chasing after so many killers when it would be so much safer to let them pass.

It was that part of him that believed in the only true law there was. Whoever had been capable of doing such a thing as murdering those people and torching their bodies had to be found. Even though they were already dead, they needed help. Their killer needed to be found.

There might have been some more to see in the vicinity, but Clint couldn't stomach any more. Not just then, anyway. The longer he stayed there, the madder he got, until he could feel the reason draining from his mind.

It wouldn't do anyone any good if he let himself get swept away by rage. That would only make him another face in the lynch mob who only cared about stringing up someone, anyone at all, just to set things right. Killing someone else by itself wasn't going to be enough to make up for what had happened.

There were some who might say that there wasn't anything at all that could be done to right a wrong like what Clint was looking at just then. Clint didn't believe in revenge, but he did believe in someone having to pay for their crime.

That was a way to help the victim's memory find some semblance of peace. And it was a way to keep the killers and thieves from running roughshod over the entire country. That was what kept surging through Clint's mind.

The only law.

As if he could read what was going on inside Clint's head, Fischer spoke up at that moment and said, "So now that you see what this is about, Mr. Adams, can I count on you to lend a hand? I can pay you for your time, if need be."

"I don't want your money," Clint answered. "But I will take you up on that offer for a place to stay and some food. That is, if that offer's still standing."

"Of course it is. That's the least I can do. What about the rest of it? I've still got a killer I need to find. Will you help me with that?"

"Yeah," Clint said as he straightened up and took another quick look at the horrific scene. "I'll help with that."

"Good."

When Clint turned around he saw that one of the other men had gotten himself to go a little closer to the carnage than the rest. He wasn't looking at the bodies or the overturned cart, however. In fact, he seemed to be doing his best not to look at any of those things. Instead he kept his eyes focused on Clint, just as he had been doing for the entire ride.

"So far this one ain't done a thing besides hold us up," the big man said without taking his eyes away from Clint.

Fischer snapped around to glare at the man who'd just spoken, with nearly enough fire in his eyes to reignite the kerosene hanging in the air. "Shut the hell up, Jonah.

When I want to hear what you have to say, I'll ask. Understand?"

Jonah opened his mouth to respond, but thought better of it and nodded instead.

Satisfied that his point had been made, Fischer turned his horse around so he could move out of the clearing. The rest of his men closed in around him.

Clint went back to where Eclipse was waiting. The Darley Arabian had instinctively backed away from the corpses as well. The stallion shook his head every now and then to try and get rid of the odors which stung his nose. It didn't seem to be doing much good, since the horse kept shifting on his feet and making uneasy noises.

"It's all right, boy," Clint said as he climbed into the saddle and then patted the stallion's neck. "We're done here for now."

As soon as Clint started to ride toward the rest of the group, Fischer waved his hand and started heading out. Just like before, some of the men rode up close to their boss, while others fanned out to the sides and let Clint through, and Jonah stayed behind to guard the rear. Clint didn't even need to look around to know he was completely surrounded. By that point of the day, he would have expected nothing else.

Fischer twisted slightly in his saddle and glanced over his shoulder. He didn't turn enough to make eye contact with Clint, but he was able to make it so his voice could be heard over the crunch of hooves against dirt and dead leaves. "My horses are tired, Mr. Adams. I don't know about you and yours, but we need to head back and get some fresh animals or else we'll be stuck out here and have to make camp."

"I should be all right for a while yet," Clint said. "If you tell me how to get to your ranch, I can search out here for a while longer and then head back to meet you there."

"The hell you will," came a voice from behind Clint.

This time, Fischer did turn all the way around so he could look directly behind him. "Jonah! What did I tell you? Jesus Christ!"

The bigger man hung his head like a scolded child and choked back a snarl meant for Clint.

"Some of my men are still a little suspicious, Mr. Adams. I'm sure you understand."

"Of course."

"You can have their help if you like."

"That won't be necessary. I've had some experience in this area, and tracking a man down is easier without someone looking over my shoulder."

Nodding, Fischer settled back into his saddle. "I intend on sending out another group as soon as I get back. The ranch is only an hour or so away." He then proceeded to give Clint directions on how to get there. It seemed simple enough, and with the lay of the land he'd seen so far, Clint figured it would be damn near impossible to miss a spread of any size once he got himself anywhere near it.

"You sure you don't want an extra hand for this job, Mr. Adams? You've seen the kind of animal we're dealing with."

"Thanks, but I can handle it. I've got a fair amount of experience with that as well."

"Yeah," Fischer said in a more quiet, reflective tone. "I've heard that about you. Bobby, tell Mr. Adams what we know about where that murderous son of a bitch might be headed. The rest of you, come along with me."

With that, Fischer snapped his reins and headed toward a fork in the trail leading to the west. Two of the others followed closely and another man broke off to come up next to Clint. That left Jonah, who took a moment to shoot Clint a bad look before riding slowly past him.

Clint could feel the threatening air surrounding the big man. It didn't bother him so much as it annoyed him, and

Clint didn't make the slightest effort to hide that fact. Once he saw that he wasn't about to back Clint down, Jonah spat on the ground and thundered off to catch up with the others.

There was no doubt in Clint's mind that he was going to be seeing that one again. More likely sooner than later.

SEVENTEEN

Bobby was the one man allowed to stay behind after Fischer had started heading back to his ranch. He was a skinny man who looked as though he was fighting to keep himself from getting swept away by the churning winds. The tattered fringe on his buckskin jacket snapped and battered his upper body. Bits of leaves and dust caught in his bristly hair.

Sharp, alert eyes stared out from beneath thick brows. The stubble on his face looked so rough that Clint almost felt sorry for the next razor that tried to clean them off. Bobby had the look of a tracker. Men like that were easy to spot since they looked as though they not only belonged in the open country but had been spit up by it.

This tracker was no exception.

"He's been heading east and southeast since he left that clearing," Bobby said in a twang that didn't belong in this part of the country. "I'd say his horse is damn near spent as well, because it's been slowing down ever since."

"Is he traveling alone?"

His mouth hung open with the words he'd been about to say. When he heard that question, however, Bobby

froze and fixed the full power of those sharp eyes upon
Clint. "What makes you ask that?"

"I didn't think it was an unreasonable question. It seems
it would take more than one man to do all the damage I
saw back there."

"Yeah. There was two of 'em at least. Maybe more."

"Maybe?"

"Nobody's seen more than that at once, but I think there
could be more'n two of 'em. They split up at the wreck
back there."

"How long ago did the . . . fire happen?" Clint felt pe-
culiar about asking the question. Mainly because the images were still fresh in his mind.

"It happened last night. Mr. Fischer found what was
left before dawn and we've been after the ones that did it
ever since. They split up and have been backtracking, but
I caught up to 'em anyhow."

"It couldn't have been easy."

"It sure as hell wasn't. Them killers know this land
almost as good as me. Damn near lost the trail more'n
once, but I picked it up again." The tracker stared at Clint
without so much scrutiny and then cocked his head to one
side. "You really him?"

"That depends on who you're talking about."

"Clint Adams. You really him?"

"Yeah. I'm him."

"I heard you killed enough men to fill a town with
souls. That true?"

"I hope not. Actually, I'm not the type to keep a tally
of such things."

Nodding, Bobby mulled whatever he was thinking inside his head and came to his own conclusions. "Well, if
I was you, I'd keep heading east. Whatever that bastard's
after, it's in that direction. There's some caves over that
way if you jog to the north once the trail cuts through a
stand of pines. Past that is some thicker woods even far-

ther north, but there's a problem with bears up that way."

"Think you can show me the last place you had his tracks?"

"Sure."

Bobby only had to ride for fifty yards or so before he started to circle and squint toward the ground. Before too long, he jumped down from his saddle, examined the earth a little closer and then motioned for Clint to join him.

"Right here," Bobby said while pointing to a patch of ground that had been dented by a horse's hoof. "They move on toward the east and then should meet up with where you saw him. Think you can take it from there?"

"I should be able to. If not, I'll take it as far as it goes and let you know the next time I see you."

"Mr. Fischer has some other fellas tracking for him, but I'm the best. It ain't pride talking. That's just the god's honest truth."

"I'm sure it is."

Bobby looked up at Clint as though he couldn't decide whether or not the last thing he'd said had been earnest or sarcastic. By the look on his face, the tracker decided to let the matter drop altogether. He strode back to his horse and leapt up onto its back. "I'll be here again with a fresh horse. I should be able to find something else before sundown."

"Hopefully, I'll have something by then as well."

"Good luck."

The words hadn't had any kind of feeling with them at all. It was just a simple farewell from a simple man. With that said, Bobby turned his horse back the way he'd come and sped away. Still concerned with his work, he made sure to wait until he was away from the tracks before letting the horse go all out.

Clint watched him go, waiting for the other man to turn and look back at him even one time. A simple gesture like that would have told him a lot. But Bobby never did look back. That told Clint a bit about the man as well.

Now that he was alone, Clint stepped over to where Bobby had been pointing and squatted down to get a closer look for himself. The spot that Bobby had shown him wasn't much to look at. That was why it took a special kind of talent to be a good tracker. A man had to know exactly what to look for, otherwise he wouldn't be able to tell a wagon rut from an old log imprint.

Clint never set out to become a tracker, but he'd picked up enough over the years to be able to find someone after they'd gone. He was looking at the print left by a horse's hoof. It was much deeper in the front and had kicked up a fairly good-sized bit of ground, which told Clint that the animal had been running.

Moving a few feet ahead, Clint found another print and then another. He could only hope that these were indeed prints left behind by the horse in question. Otherwise, he might just find himself tracking down Mr. Fischer or any one of the others that had been riding with him.

Before he moved on, Clint spotted something odd about the print that he had almost overlooked. The end of the horseshoe was cracked right at the tip. Perhaps that had been the factor that made Bobby so sure he was on the right path.

Clint made a note of that before he got back to where Eclipse was waiting. He had plenty of other places to go and not a lot of time to get there.

EIGHTEEN

Clint made sure to give the tracks a wide berth. Although he didn't plan on following them all the way from that spot, he didn't want to ride all over them either. Instead, he headed back to the rise where he'd last seen that first rider. There was a fair amount of ground to cover, but Eclipse had had some time to catch his breath and was more than up to the task.

It felt to Clint as though he was riding over the same ground for the hundredth time that day as he thundered over the trail and sliced through the winds. By the time he was back where all the day's events had started, the sun was hiding behind a thick bank of clouds. It wouldn't be too much longer before darkness began to creep in, and Clint didn't know how Fischer planned on getting more searchers out before nightfall.

But rather than try to figure out the silver-haired man, Clint kept himself focused on his own task. Eyeballing his position as best he could, Clint circled the open land between the rise and the stretch of trees, trying to find approximately where he'd been when he'd first heard those gunshots.

It wasn't an easy task by a long shot, but he did reach

a point where everything around him seemed to snap into place. He looked around for a bit until he picked up the tracks of several horses. Clint didn't bother trying to sift through them all, but instead looked only for an imprint with that one unusual shoe.

Sure enough, he found it no more than ten yards from where he'd started. With that done, Clint climbed back into the saddle and snapped the reins. Eclipse launched himself toward the edge of the rise and Clint steered him all the way around it, until he'd run more than half of its length. Clint slowed the Darley Arabian and then swung down to the ground, jogging over to where he'd found the rider hiding.

Going a little ways past that, he found the space that had been flattened out by the horse. He was careful not to take one wrong step that might possibly mar something of value. Again, it didn't take long to find what he was looking for.

Seeing that odd print there sealed it up in Clint's mind. Those tracks most definitely belonged to that rider's horse. Now that he had that firmly in mind, he could track the rider on his own without worrying if he'd been thrown off course by a wrong assumption.

Clint was just about to mount up again when he heard something that made him freeze right where he was. The sound wasn't much louder than the rattle of the tree limbs or the rustle of leaves, but it was sharp enough to catch his attention. It was a loud snapping that could only have been made by something heavy breaking a piece of brittle wood beneath it.

The sound was unmistakable and so was the realization that came along with it.

Someone was close by.

Judging by the direction the sound had come from, that someone was in the thick bunch of trees that provided some of the only cover to be had behind the rise.

Clint had only been still for a second or two, which was enough for him to come to a few decisions. First of all, it probably wasn't Bobby following him, since any tracker worth his salt would never slip up by alerting his target like that.

Second, whoever it was doing the following was eager to get as close to Clint as possible, since he should have been able to keep an eye on him right from where he was.

That left one main possibility in Clint's mind. He filed it away for the moment and kept walking back to where Eclipse was standing. If he was right about who was tailing him, Clint hadn't given away enough signs for the other man to suspect that he'd been discovered. In fact, Clint could almost picture the smug grin that was surely creeping onto the other man's face right about now.

Once he was back in the saddle, Clint got Eclipse moving at a brisk walk until he was out of the trees. From there, he snapped the reins and the stallion responded by breaking into a gallop.

Clint rode as fast as he could go without having to worry about endangering himself or Eclipse. The Darley Arabian bolted through the stand of trees, leaping over the occasional fallen log or exposed root. He broke out of the trees just as he was coming to the end of the rise, and as soon as he could, Clint took a hard right, which brought him around the edge.

From there, Clint pulled back on the reins, slowing Eclipse just enough for him to be able to jump from the saddle without breaking his neck. It wasn't the best landing he could have hoped for, but Clint was able to drop to the ground and into a short sideways roll to cushion himself. Eclipse naturally followed him, and when Clint came back up to his feet, he slapped the Darley Arabian lightly on the rump, which was the horse's signal to keep running.

Clint didn't look back. Instead, he ran up the rise a few

paces until he just crested over the top. It wasn't too high, since he'd started climbing at the very end of the ridge, but when he looked over to the other side, Clint figured he'd gotten himself about eight or ten feet above the bottom of the rise.

As the sound of Eclipse's steps began to fade away, another sound began to make itself known. Clint could hear it like a quickly approaching storm, and the longer he waited, the louder it got. Keeping himself low, he followed the new sound back to its source and grinned when he saw that his first guess about who had been behind him had been right.

Sure enough, Jonah rode between the trees wearing a smile of his own. By the looks of it, he must have thought that he'd been following Clint without tipping his hand one bit. In fact, the big man didn't even look anywhere near where Clint was hiding. As far as he knew, he simply had to follow the sound of Eclipse's hooves.

Clint turned his back on Jonah and began scooting down his side of the rise. He could hear the big man coming and could even feel Jonah's horse pounding against the earth. By the time Jonah had rounded the corner, Clint was crouched and ready to make his move.

NINETEEN

Jonah raced by, passing within ten feet of Clint's position. As soon as he had gone, Clint stood up and let out a piercing whistle that sliced through the air like an arrow.

Several yards away, Eclipse's ears pricked up, and he came to a halt. The stallion turned and started running back toward where that familiar call had come from.

The big man that had been riding up behind the Darley Arabian pricked up as well. He straightened in the saddle and twisted around so far to look toward the sound of the whistle that he damn near threw himself out of the saddle. He pulled back hard on his own reins, and it took all his strength to keep the horse from rearing up and tossing him off its back.

Clint had hoped to create a distraction, but hadn't even thought it would go so well. He took his time picking a new spot and got himself settled in behind a sizeable boulder wedged into the side of the rise. As soon as he saw Jonah turn to get a look at him, Clint shouted, "What's the matter? Doesn't Fischer trust me to work alone?"

It took Jonah a couple more seconds before he could settle his horse and zero in on where Clint's voice was coming from. Once he had Clint in his sights, the big man dug his heels into his horse's sides and started immediately into a charge.

Clint knew that Jonah wasn't too fond of him and even thought that Fischer had good reason not to be too trusting of every stranger he happened across. But he hadn't been expecting Jonah to attack him as soon as he got a look at him.

Even with the other man coming at him from a distance, Clint could see the murderous intent etched into Jonah's face. He still held his ground, however, confident that he had the upper hand. Besides, Clint figured he still had another couple seconds before Jonah's horse could reach him. That would be enough time to see if the bigger man meant business or was only trying to put a scare into him.

"What are you doing?" Clint shouted. "If this is just because I tricked you a little bit here, then I think you might be overreacting just a b—"

Jonah had gotten to Clint's position by then and snapped his reins just enough to get his horse's front legs off the ground. The animal launched itself into a jump that would have taken it over Clint's boulder without much room to spare.

Of course, Clint was still standing behind that boulder, and he would have been knocked into next week if he hadn't flattened himself behind the rock at precisely the last second.

Even though he knew he was going to have to move or be killed by that charging animal, Clint could hardly believe that it was actually happening. Most horses wouldn't even jump headfirst into something like that, and most riders certainly weren't in the practice of trying to get them to do so.

But where most men would have turned away or backed off, Jonah had thundered right ahead. If nothing else, Clint had to give the man credit for that.

Crouching down until his knees were jammed into his face, Clint pressed his side against the boulder and tensed every muscle in his body as he heard Jonah's horse sail over him. When the animal's front hooves hit the ground behind him, Clint swore the impact was enough to pop him off the ground at least an inch. He thought he was in for a world of hurt when he felt something touch the middle of his back and slide down.

If that horse was able to dig a hind foot into Clint's spine, he knew crippled would be the best result he could hope for. In reality, dead was more of what he'd be looking at.

That was indeed the horse's hind foot, but it only managed to graze Clint's back before pounding into the ground directly behind him. The animal thundered onward a couple more paces and let out a whinny that rattled inside of Clint's ears.

As soon as he knew the animal had passed him by, Clint stood up and waited for pain to stab at him from one of the bones that must have been broken. But even though he'd come less than a hair's width away from being trampled, he'd somehow managed to make it through with only a throbbing bruise on his back and ribs.

The world seemed to have slowed down for that instant, giving Clint an opportunity to pull himself together and react to what had just happened. At the very least, his near miss just then had shown him what kind of man he was truly dealing with.

Every emotion in Clint's head shouted for him to drop the big man from his saddle with a bullet through the back of his head. But that was simple rage talking, and Clint had plenty of experience looking past that. His hand dropped to the Colt at his side and plucked the weapon from its holster in a single, smooth motion. Less that a second later, he'd taken aim and fired just as Jonah was turning his horse back around to face him.

The Colt barked once, sending a chunk of hot lead flying through the air. The bullet hissed past the horse's face, clipping off a few hairs and just enough skin to draw a trickle of blood. The wound wasn't much worse than something the horse might have gotten riding through a thorn bush, but it put one hell of a scare into the animal, which was why Clint had fired it.

Before it could build up enough speed for a second charge, Jonah's horse dug its hooves into the ground, reared slightly and turned sharp enough to shake the man off its back. Jonah tried to hang on, but the movement was too sudden and too powerful for him to resist, and he suddenly found himself toppling through empty air.

Clint's blood was pumping so quickly through his veins that he was almost next to Jonah before the bigger man could finish his fall. Apart from the dull thump of Jonah hitting the ground, Clint could hear the wet snap of a bone breaking.

"That's enough, Jonah," Clint snarled. "There's not even a reason for any of this."

"The hell there isn't." Jonah's voice was thick with pain, and before he finished his reply, his foot was already stabbing up and out toward Clint's stomach.

TWENTY

Clint had tested the big man once and was surprised with the result. Only a fool would have let himself be surprised twice, and Clint was sure as hell not a fool. He'd prepared himself for just about anything, even though the other man had been thrown from his horse.

He noticed Jonah's kick just as it was starting, and his body moved reflexively in response. Twisting on the ball of one foot, Clint spun ninety degrees to one side, allowing the big man's boot to sail past him. Clint lifted the Colt and brought its handle down sharply onto Jonah's shin. The impact was good enough that even Clint winced.

Jonah gritted his teeth and let out a noise that was equal parts profanity and growl. He'd only used one hand to prop himself up, and the other was already grabbing for a scabbard at his belt.

Knowing that he'd hit the other man's leg pretty hard, Clint could hardly believe it when that same leg not only stayed right where it was, but came hooking around toward him yet again. It was a clumsy kick, but just quick enough to catch Clint right above the waist. Jonah's heel dug into his ribs, sending sharp bolts of pain through Clint's lower body.

Rather than let himself get too distracted by the blow, Clint let it fuel him to move even faster. By the way things were going, he was going to need every bit of speed he could muster. Jonah was proving to be a more capable opponent with each passing second.

Seeing Clint's eyes leave him for a second, Jonah pulled the knife from his scabbard and flipped it so that he held its blade between his fingers. He rolled to one side to keep from getting hit again, and as soon as he lined himself up the right way, he snapped his hand forward and let the blade fly from his hand.

Clint almost didn't spot the blade coming at him until it was too late. As it was, the sun was at just the right angle to catch the metal with a stray beam of light, which glinted for less than half a second. Reacting immediately to the sight of the weapon in Jonah's hand, Clint twisted his upper body and lowered his gun hand.

The blade left Jonah's fingers and had enough time to make half a turn. By the time it completed that single turn, it would be buried deep inside Clint's flesh.

Clint's modified pistol barked once more. Like a surgeon aiming to cut precisely on target, Clint's eyes focused on where he wanted the bullet to go. The round cleared the Colt's barrel and struck dead-on, sparking against polished metal as it ricocheted off the knife's blade in midair and hissed off in another direction. Steel fragments spun through the air like a small, glittering explosion.

A few of the metal chips dug into Clint's arm, just as a few wedged themselves beneath Jonah's skin. The knife itself wobbled awkwardly as it was redirected by the bullet, and landed on its side ten feet from either man's reach.

Amazingly, for a man his size, Jonah was still about to launch himself into his next move when he felt the bottom of Clint's boot slam squarely against his chest. Some of the breath was knocked from his lungs as his back hit the ground. Reflexively, his hands started to grab for Clint's foot.

Leaning forward, Clint put more of his weight behind the foot he had pressed against Jonah's chest. He managed to push the bigger man down simply because he had gravity and leverage working on his side. He knew that could change in a heartbeat, though.

"I don't want to kill you," Clint said as he leveled the Colt so that Jonah was staring straight down its barrel. "But I will if you don't leave me any choice."

That was enough to stop the big man before he could make his next move. His chest heaved beneath Clint's boot and his hands were already taking hold of Clint's ankle. When he saw the single, black eye of the gun barrel looking back at him, however, he slowly moved his hands back and let himself be pushed flat against the ground.

Clint took his foot off of him and stepped around so that he was standing next to Jonah's head. "All right now," he said, placing the toe of his left foot against the other man's forehead. "Tell me what brought all this on."

"Just following orders."

"Fischer's orders?"

Even with Clint all but stepping on his head, Jonah managed to get a snide look on his face. "It sure wasn't the President."

"Now's not the time for smart-ass comments." Looking up, Clint studied the sky for a moment and added, "In fact, now's not even the time for this conversation."

"Good. Then I'll meet up with you later, Adams."

Now it was Clint's turn to wear the sarcastic grin. "No. You'll wait right here and take a little nap. Maybe after that you won't be so cranky."

Straining against the bottom of Clint's boot, Jonah lifted his head up off the ground. "A nap? What the f—"

Jonah's voice stopped abruptly as Clint stomped his

foot down just hard enough to smack the back of his head against the hard, rocky ground. Blind rage flashed in the big man's eyes, but that only lasted for a split second, until unconsciousness dimmed the light in his skull altogether.

Clint turned around and saw that Eclipse was waiting only a few feet away. He called the Darley Arabian over and fetched some rope that was hanging from his saddle. After trussing Jonah up like a calf in a rodeo, Clint secured the other end of the rope to a petrified stump rising a little ways up the incline.

Although Jonah's horse was still awfully spooked, Clint managed to coax the animal near a tree where it could be tied off. The horse didn't seem to mind waiting there just as long as nobody was shooting at it anymore.

Even though the nick on the horse's head was no longer bleeding, Clint felt twice as bad for putting it there as he did for any of the pain he'd caused Jonah. He patted the horse behind the ears as a quick apology and then headed back to Eclipse.

Before climbing up into the saddle, Clint picked up Jonah's damaged blade and dropped it into one of his bags. He didn't think the big man would be held forever in that spot, but Clint didn't need the bonds to last that long anyway.

TWENTY-ONE

Clint didn't have too far to go, but he didn't have much time to get there. His reunion with Jonah hadn't been too long, but it had used up valuable daylight. The sun was now beginning to sink further past the horizon, and the sky was turning a rich shade of purple and red. As beautiful as it may have been, Clint saw those colors as a kind of hourglass that had been turned on its end for too long.

He'd started Eclipse running full speed because he knew the Darley Arabian didn't have a lot of steam left. The stallion gave Clint everything he had and would have kept on trying if necessary. But Clint wasn't about to harm the animal when he could just as easily make his way in the dark.

Of course, "easy" probably wasn't the best choice of words, but anything would be easier than trying to get along without Eclipse. Clint knew where he was headed and could see the woods that the first rider had told him about just as the light began to drain from the sky.

It was dark when Clint rode into the woods, and he was straining his eyes to get a good look at the trail in front of him. Eclipse was moving right along, but his steps weren't as solid as they'd been earlier. The stallion was

83

breathing heavy and Clint had no choice but to swing down from the saddle and lead the animal by the reins.

From the lower vantage point, Clint had an easier time seeing the path. Before too long, his eyes had adjusted enough to the darkness that he could even make out the forest around him. But if there had been more clouds in the sky to obscure the silvery light coming down from the stars, Clint would have been totally blind.

He could see the shapes surrounding him as though every object had been dusted with luminescent powder. Apart from the occasional flutter of wings or scurrying of unseen feet, the woods were almost completely quiet. The main noise that Clint could detect was the flow of wind among the loose, dead leaves. But that sound had become so familiar he barely even heard it anymore.

Using his memory and instinct as his main guide, Clint kept himself heading as close to north as he could figure. He was just beginning to feel uneasy with his inner sense of direction when he saw a large, ominous shape looming a little ways off the path.

The shape reminded him of a large mouth opening up from a head buried in the earth. Since that head would have been bigger than anything possible, Clint knew that he'd finally found the cave that he'd been looking for. As he made his way to the opening, he still couldn't shake the image of that giant mouth from his brain. At times like these, it was easy to see how more primitive men started up legends of monsters and gods moving through the forests at night.

Clint never did believe in such things as monsters, but he jumped all the same when he saw something move suddenly from the opening of that giant mouth. His hand went reflexively for his gun, and he took on a lower, more defensive posture.

"Adams?" came a somewhat familiar voice from the cave opening. "Is that you?"

Slowly, Clint's body began to relax. Even so, he still kept his gun in hand. "It's me. Come up here where I can see you better."

The shape that Clint made out was no monster, but was most definitely a man. The figure came forward slowly with both hands raised in the air. "I'm the one that told you how to get here, remember? I said I'd wait for you at this here cave."

With his ribs continuing to ache from the last time he'd let someone get within arm's reach of him, Clint felt the hackles still raised on the back of his neck. Perhaps it was the woods playing on those inborn fears, making him instinctually uneasy. The other man still didn't seem to pose any threat, but Clint was in the frame of mind where it was better to be safe than sorry.

"I heard some of the things Mr. Fischer was saying to you," the other man said. "And I want to thank you for coming. Truth be told, I thought for sure you'd either come back to hunt me down or send the law after me."

"That still might be the case," Clint said. "I haven't decided yet."

"Fair enough."

Once the other man was close enough for Clint to make out a few details on his face, he saw that the guy wasn't holding a weapon and seemed just as nervous as Clint felt. Holstering the Colt, Clint said, "After all this trouble to get here, I still don't even know your name."

"It's Tanner. Mark Tanner. Now how about we get inside before we wake up something bigger than your horse?"

TWENTY-TWO

The opening of the cave stretched up to only an inch or so over Clint's head. He took his hat off just to make sure it didn't get swept off as he walked inside. Eclipse could get in just far enough to be inside the cave before he had to stop and find a comfortable place to stand. There was another horse there already, which belonged to Mark Tanner. As soon as Eclipse realized he didn't have to walk anymore, he dropped his head low and got some much needed rest.

Tanner led Clint farther inside the cave, to a spot where it looked like he'd started building a campfire. By the incomplete stack of kindling, he hadn't been at the task for very long. Sitting down next to the pile of wood, Tanner rearranged the kindling until it looked like something that might actually hold a spark.

"I haven't been here too long myself," Tanner said. "But this is a good place to spend a night or two. Once I get a fire going, it'll be downright comfortable."

"I can do without comfort," Clint said sharply. "I'd much rather have some answers."

"Answers?" Tanner asked without looking up from his

86

stack of twigs and branches. "I'll see what I can do if you want to ask the questions."

"Let's start first off with why those men were chasing you."

"I told you that already."

"Yeah. You said they were bandits trying to steal from you and your friend. There was also something about them threatening your lives, wasn't there?"

Digging in his shirt pocket, Tanner pulled out a couple matches and started striking them against the stone floor near his feet. "Do you even have to ask if they were trying to kill me? I thought you could tell that much by seeing what you saw."

Clint sat down as well, keeping his back pressed up against the wall of the cave. He watched Tanner go through the process of lighting a match and then touching the little flame to the kindling. He then got the flame to grow until there was a decent fire crackling on the floor of the cave.

The entire process took a couple minutes, and when it was finished, Clint spoke in a voice that seemed to cut straight through all the way to the back of the stone cavern. "How about you cut the bullshit, Mark. Either you start dealing straight with me or I walk out of here right now and come back with the law."

Tanner looked surprised, but only for a moment. He let out a breath and stared down at the growing fire. "What did Fischer tell you?"

"He told me a lot of things. How about you start off first by telling me about what he showed me."

"What was that?"

"You know goddamn well what I'm talking about," Clint shot back. "I've been through too much today to be put through any more."

"I suppose he took you to that wagon wreck in the woods."

"Yeah. Tell me about that wreck."

"I wasn't even on that wagon when it pulled away from Mr. Fischer's ranch. It stopped off in Sharpeston to take on supplies, and I got on there."

It took Clint a moment to think, but eventually he remembered that Sharpeston was the name of the closest town in the area. It was about a day's ride south and was a trading post that he knew mostly for a particularly wild saloon that had sprouted up there. Any town that catered to cowboys or trappers looking to spend their money had its fair share of wild saloons. Last time Clint had been through Sharpeston, it wasn't much more than a group of shacks in the middle of a dozen tents.

"So tell me again where the bandits fit into all of this," Clint said. "That's one of the things I'd really like to hear."

Unable to look Clint in the eyes, Tanner poked a stick into the fire a couple times and shrugged his shoulders. "Maybe I might have stretched the truth about that."

"Stretched the truth or made it up completely?"

Tanner's head snapped up, and he looked as though he was about to spring to his feet as well. "That bastard was trying to steal from me! And he was trying to kill me as well. It's just that I didn't have enough time to tell you everything, what with him and his men breathing down my neck with guns blazing."

"Well, we've got some time now," Clint said. "Let's hear it."

While Tanner had started to look riled up a moment ago, the heat in his eyes died down almost immediately then, and he went back to stirring the fire. "We'll still need more time than we've got right now if you want to hear the whole story."

"I don't want to hear the whole story," Clint pointed out. "Just the parts that ended with me putting my neck on the line."

"If there's any way I can make it up to you, just name it. I know I owe you my life and I'll never forget that."

"Then start with that wagon wreck," Clint said in a tone that didn't sound quite as harsh. "Tell me what happened."

"Jesus," Tanner said in a faraway voice that made it seem as though he'd forgotten Clint was there with him. "It seems like it all started so long ago. I met Mr. Fischer a couple summers ago. I used to work with a prospector down in Colorado who also made some extra money by running supplies to ranchers and such.

"Mr. Fischer offered me a job running supplies just for him, as well as some other odd jobs, and I took it. The money was good, and at the time, that was really all I cared about."

Listening to that, Clint felt as though he'd heard those same words before. The truth was that he had heard those same words, or something very close to them, coming out of the mouths of more regretful men than he could remember. Even if those situations had turned out all right, the road leading up to the end was never easy.

"What kind of odd jobs are you talking about?" Clint asked.

Tanner paused for a second, staring into the fire as though he was watching the whole thing play out amid the flames. "Mostly transporting. Supplies and passengers. There were shipments to be delivered, but I never really knew what they were. It wasn't my business to ask."

"So that means you knew it was something besides dry goods."

Reluctantly, Tanner nodded. "I figured. But it couldn't have been anything too bad. There was never any trouble along the way, and nobody seemed concerned about what was going on. Even the law in town didn't seem to care. It was just business as usual."

"And how long did that last?"

"A year. In that time, I started getting business of my own to worry about. I'd meet up with folks in town who had jobs for me. They'd heard about me or met me through Mr. Fischer and knew I was a trustworthy man. I'm a hard worker, Mr. Adams. All I wanted was to make a way for myself and get some land of my own someday.

"This was around the time that I met up with Alex Wright. He met up with me several times outside of Sharpeston and drove Mr. Fischer's shipments on to wherever they needed to go. It was his idea to branch out for ourselves."

"And you were the inside man," Clint said, refusing to let himself be lulled into the innocent picture of himself that Tanner was trying to paint.

Tanner nodded. "That's right. Mr. Fischer trusted me and he said that he'd help me start my own business if I wanted. I thought it was about time to take him up on that offer. Me and Alex had a setup and I was supposed to meet a friend of mine from the old days once I got on my own."

"Who's this friend?"

"Name's Chris Sorenson. He was supposed to make sure me, Alex and the others got out all right."

"Fischer said something about his daughter getting hurt. What happened with her?"

"The hell if I know. I didn't think he had any children."

TWENTY-THREE

Tanner rubbed his eyes. "I don't know about no daughter. There was a woman there that Mr. Fischer protected like she belonged to him."

"What's her name?" Clint asked.

Tilting his head, Tanner smiled to himself as though the very act of thinking about this woman was enough to brighten his mood. "Kimberly. She's the prettiest thing you'd ever seen."

"So you ran afoul of this girl, and that didn't sit too well with your boss," Clint said, trying to speed up the other man's tale.

"Kimberly is a hot little lady, Mr. Adams. I'm sure a man like you has met plenty of them. When I was around her, I couldn't help myself. She's sweet as candy and didn't mind giving me a taste now and then."

"Fischer said you raped her."

Tanner's eyes darted up from the fire and locked onto Clint. For a moment, it looked as though he was going to throw himself over the flames just so he could get his hands around Clint's neck. "That's a load of horse manure," Tanner snarled. "If anything, she raped me."

"Well, that's not what Fischer thinks."

"You shouldn't believe all you hear, then. I would think a man like you would know that as well."

Tanner watched Clint for those moments and moved back slightly, as though he could read the other man's thoughts. "He's saying I killed those folks, isn't he?"

Clint nodded. "And worse."

"Jesus. I'm a dead man."

"Not just yet. What happened with that overturned wagon I saw? You said you were on that when it left the ranch?"

Once again, Tanner's eyes lowered down to the fire. Looking at the flames seemed to calm him enough to go on. He took whatever he needed from the fire and then let out a slow breath. "I got on after it pulled out. I met up with the rest outside of Mr. Fischer's spread."

"Why?"

"Because he was already looking for me by then."

"It sounded like you and Fischer were on good terms. Why the sudden change of heart?"

"Because that's the way things go, Mr. Adams. I'm sure that a—"

"Yeah," Clint interrupted. "A man like me knows that happens every now and again."

Laughing quietly, Tanner picked up the stick he'd been using to prod the fiery pieces of wood and started up where he'd left off. "Me and Fischer were on good enough terms, but that was getting sour. I didn't know just how sour until I was on that cart yesterday and those . . ." He trailed off there, suddenly losing the strength to keep talking.

Tanner pulled in another breath and let his eyes wander among the crackling fire. "We were driving through the woods on that cart you saw. Me, two other workers from the spread and Ellen."

Although he'd been trying to hold it back, Clint was unable to stop himself from picturing those burnt bodies.

When he heard the woman's name, he got a distinct vision of that charred corpse wrapped up in her melted dress. "Fischer said that was his sister."

Suddenly, the cave was filled with a shuddering moan that sounded like tortured spirits from those monster stories Clint had been thinking about upon his arrival. The sound was coming from outside the cave, and as it spilled into the stone walls, it spread out and bounced around like a moth trapped inside a jar.

TWENTY-FOUR

The moans went through Clint's skull, playing briefly upon the primitive part of his mind that was still afraid of the dark. That was something he couldn't control and it only lasted a split second. Only animals let themselves be ruled by such impulses. Clint used them as a way to stoke his own fires, get him up and onto his feet.

In a blur of motion, Clint was away from the fire and moving toward the front of the cave. Tanner was right behind him, lunging first for a pile that Clint had hardly noticed before. The other man's hands went beneath a folded coat and saddlebag, to emerge holding an old Army model pistol.

Clint watched him from the corner of his eye, his hand on his own gun in case Tanner was about to try anything stupid. But the only thing that seemed to be on Tanner's mind was getting his pistol and heading outside. Just to be safe, Clint kept him in sight as he jogged into the night.

It wasn't too hard at all to find out where those sounds were coming from. By the time he and Tanner stepped outside, the moans had turned into a scream, which eventually formed into words.

"Mark," it said. "If you're there, you've got to help me."

That was all Tanner needed to hear before he took off like a rabbit being chased by a pack of wolves. Clint followed on his heels, listening for any other sounds besides the other voice. The winds had actually died down for a change and Clint could hear heavy footsteps coming his way. Since those footsteps were more than likely being made by the same one doing the screaming, Clint was fairly sure that the new arrival was alone.

Of course, that didn't mean he wasn't still being followed.

"Mr. Adams, come here quick!"

Following Tanner's voice, Clint ran ahead another few yards to find Tanner crouching down over a body laying on its side. Clint thought they were both too late to help the third man, but then the body twitched and started struggling to get up.

Tanner looked up at Clint with wide, worried eyes. "It's Sorenson, Mr. Adams. We've got to help him. He's hurt."

Sorenson looked up at Clint. There was suspicion written all over his pale face, but he was too weak to say what was on his mind. After crying out for help, he barely seemed to have enough energy to lift his arms. He did manage to get one arm wrapped around Tanner's neck, but couldn't even move his legs once he was lifted up off the ground.

Taking hold of the fallen man's other arm, Clint looped it around his shoulders and added his strength to Tanner's. Together, they lifted Sorenson up and carried him between them back to the cave. Once inside, they lowered him down so that he was sitting with his back against the wall.

Now Clint could see the true extent of Sorenson's injuries. It had been obvious by the noises he made that he was hurt, and Clint had picked up the familiar smell of blood. After setting him down, Clint looked at Sorenson and immediately spotted the dark stain that had soaked through the front of his shirt.

All of Sorenson's upper body was painted the dark crimson of blood. So much had soaked into his clothes that it looked almost black and oily. It was hard to tell where the blood was coming from or even how many wounds there were. Kneeling down, Clint started peeling open the other man's shirt.

"This is going to hurt," Clint said. "But we've got to see what's going on here. What can you tell me?"

Sorenson started to talk, but then let out his breath in a rush of air that seemed to deflate his entire torso. "Who is this?" he asked Tanner. "Is he . . . one of Fischer's?"

Tanner helped open Sorenson's shirt. "Don't worry," he told the wounded man. "We can trust him a hell of a lot more than any of Fischer's men."

"Are . . . are you sure about that?"

Suddenly, Tanner looked over to Clint as though he was seeing him for the first time. It seemed as though he was unsure as to whether or not he could trust Clint after all. Finally, he came to some kind of middle ground inside his head. "He's not one of Fischer's men. We can trust him."

It didn't take an expert at reading people to know that Tanner was more sure about the first of his statements than the second. Clint didn't mind Tanner's suspicions. In fact, he still had plenty of his own to keep him busy. For the moment, however, Clint concerned himself more with the man in front of him, who was wearing most of his blood on his shirt.

As he pulled apart Sorenson's shirt, Clint could see what he'd been hoping not to. There wasn't one bullet hole in the other man's chest. There wasn't even two. Clint counted three holes in all; one just above and to the right of Sorenson's waist, one through his stomach and another in the vicinity of his heart.

"Oh my god," Tanner said as he saw the wounds for himself. "Who did this to you?"

Sorenson was paler than a sheet and was losing the fire in his eyes. The color of his skin became chalky, and his eyes started to glaze over as though he was going blind but was still looking around, at things no one else could see. He turned his face toward his friend, but his eyes were still gazing straight through him.

"It's . . . not as . . . bad as it looks," Sorenson croaked.

Clint knew that was true. If it was as bad as it looked, the other man wouldn't have even made it this far. But that didn't change the fact that Sorenson was dying. There wasn't anything on earth that could stop it now. Clint wasn't a doctor, but a man like him had seen that kind of thing plenty of times before.

Tanner tried looking into his friend's eyes, but quickly saw that Sorenson couldn't see him. He then looked up to Clint. "Can't you do anything?"

Not knowing exactly what to say, Clint met Tanner's pleading stare and simply shook his head.

At first, Tanner looked angry, but then he took another look at his friend and knew Clint wasn't the one to blame. He wanted to comfort Sorenson by patting his shoulder or somehow letting him know he was still there, but he couldn't find a place on him that wasn't coated in blood.

"Who did this?" Tanner asked, placing his hand on Sorenson's shoulder. "Did you get a look at who shot you?"

"Didn't see anything but a shadow," Sorenson said. By the look in his eyes, he seemed to be describing something from a dream. "Thought it was a bear."

Leaning forward to hear whatever else Sorenson was going to say, Tanner stared down at his friend without moving an inch. A couple seconds went by before Soren-

son's eyes made that uncanny shift that would haunt anyone who'd ever seen it.

There wasn't any real movement or even a blink. Instead, the wounded man's eyes just sort of emptied, until
they appeared to be nothing but dirty glass orbs. When
that happened, Sorenson let out a final breath which tapered off to nothingness.

It was that moment in which some people say the soul
leaves a body. Clint didn't know about that for sure, but
it was certainly easier to believe in spirits when he heard
that breath for himself.

Tanner stared down at Sorenson, shaking him gently at
first but then grabbing him by the shoulders and rattling
the body when he didn't get an answer. "Jesus Christ,"
he said after letting go of the body and getting to his feet.
Tanner looked at the blood on his hands and then over to
Clint. "He's dead. He's really dead."

Clint stood up and walked back to the fire, where he'd
left his hat. After dropping it onto his head, he moved
over to where Eclipse was waiting.

"Sorenson is gone, Mr. Adams. What am I gonna do
now?"

"Bury him," Clint said. "And stay here. I've got an
appointment to keep."

TWENTY-FIVE

It didn't sit too well in Clint's gut the way he'd left Tanner standing over the body of his friend. Then again, there wasn't anything that could have happened in that moment to make Clint feel any better. The truth of the matter was that he still didn't know the entire story of what was going on, and there was plenty more that didn't sit well with him.

Tanner's own words drifted through his mind just then.

A man like you probably sees that kind of thing an awful lot.

Clint shook his head. If only that wasn't so damn true. Over the years, he'd become an expert in being dropped into powderkegs and having to find the way out. He never did know all of what was going on right off the bat, because he was never the one to start those messes. Unfortunately, he was real good at cleaning them up. Perhaps that was why he found himself in so many powderkegs.

After leading Eclipse through the thickest part of the woods, Clint climbed onto the stallion's back and snapped the reins. He wasn't about to push Eclipse too hard, but he needed to go faster than a walk. With his eyes adjusted to the darkness, Clint managed to find his way back onto

the trail which would lead him to the spot where Jonah
was hopefully still waiting for him.

As he rode, Clint wondered if he should have taken
measures to make sure that Tanner didn't cut and run as
soon as he was able. It looked as though that horse inside
the cave had been too tired to do much of anything, which
was one thing in Clint's favor. The only other thing he
could count on was the fact that Tanner was indeed going
to bury Sorenson's body that night. After that was finished, Tanner would more than likely stay put until morning. After all, he'd looked almost as dead tired as his
horse.

If Tanner was going to try to run away, then that wasn't
any of Clint's concern. Clint's own instincts were to trust
that Tanner would at least stay in or near that cave for a
day or two. Besides, if Fischer was so intent on finding
him, then Tanner wouldn't have many places to run anyway.

The one person that Clint knew would use the first opportunity to get away from him was Jonah. He was fairly
confident in the strength of his knots, but Clint wasn't
about to assume they would hold the big man forever.
There was still plenty to ask Tanner, but that would have
to wait. The more time that passed, the less likely it would
be that Fischer would have anything to do with Clint once
he showed up.

Clint wanted to get a word or two with Fischer as well
as check out as much of both men's stories as possible.
To do that, he needed to meet with Fischer and see his
ranch. There was also someone else that he wanted to
meet and Kimberly Fischer was her name. At least, Clint
hoped that was her name, since Tanner didn't seem to
know of any other woman who would fit the bill.

Whatever she was calling herself, Clint needed to see
her.

Clint thought about all of this as he rode southwest

back toward the all-too-familiar rise. The moon and stars
didn't give off more than a glimmer of light, but that was
all Clint needed to spot the land formation he'd been seek-
ing. Eclipse had kept up a fairly good pace and made the
trip in less time than Clint had anticipated. Just thinking
about the Darley Arabian made Clint feel guilty for driving the animal so hard.

He scratched the stallion's ears as a silent promise to
make up for the grueling day. Eclipse seemed tired as hell,
but still kept on running as long as he felt the reins moving down his back. When Clint pulled back on the leather
straps, the stallion let out a deep snort and pawed the
ground next to a large, unmoving figure laying beside a
stump.

The sudden sound and movement caused the figure to
jump, but only a little. After that little bit of motion, the
figure became still once again. There was hardly even any
smoky breath coming from his nostrils.

"Come on, Jonah," Clint said as he dropped heavily
from the saddle and landed a respectable distance from
the big man's arms or legs. "I know you're not sleeping,
and I sure as hell know I didn't kill you. Sit up and make
this easier for both of us."

Even though the ropes looked to be intact, Clint wasn't
about to walk blindly up to the other man. He could still
feel painful reminders from the last scuffle he'd had.

When he didn't get a reply right away, Clint drew his
Colt and snapped back the hammer just to make sure Jonah had something good to hear. "All right then," he said.
"Since I somehow managed to lose this one, I might as
well put a few rounds into him just to make sure there
isn't any pain. Too bad. I was just getting to like him."

"Fuck you, Adams," Jonah grunted as he curled up into
a sitting position. The ropes were still holding, but they
appeared to be frayed in a few places. Wriggling himself
so that he was upright with his legs bent in front of him,

Jonah moved fairly well considering just how restrained he was.

"That's no way to talk to someone who came all the way back to help a man in need."

"But that's a good way to talk to you, asshole," Jonah replied. "If you knew what was good for you, you'd put them bullets into me now. I sure as hell won't hesitate the next time I get my chance."

"I'm sure you won't. Now, do you want to get out of here, or would you rather curse at me some more?"

"Where do you think we're headed, Adams? How far do you think you're gonna get before the rest of the boys find us? I'll bet they're gonna be here anytime now."

"Actually, I was counting on that very thing. We can make sure they find us sooner if we ride toward them. You have any suggestions on the quickest way to cross their path?"

Jonah looked up at him, and even in the dark, Clint could see the anger and confusion on his face. Gritting his teeth, the bigger man shifted on the ground and then nodded over his shoulder toward the rise.

"Head east," Jonah said. "You know that's the way they headed when they left you."

"Yeah, I know," Clint said as he dropped his Colt into its holster and fastened the little strap locking it into place. "But you should also know that if you make one move I don't like, I'll gun you down and consider it self-defense. Understand?"

"Sure."

"Good. Now let's get you onto your horse so we can get moving. I'm looking forward to that bed and food Fischer promised me."

"You gonna untie me?"

Clint laughed and reached down to take hold of Jonah's wrist. "If it's all the same to you, I think I'll risk throwing out my back getting your carcass up into that saddle. Nice try, though."

"Hey. You can't blame a man for trying."

Even though it was awkward and difficult getting Jonah to his feet and over to his horse, those moments were the first time since they'd met that Clint didn't think the big man was intent on killing him. Not that they were about to start swapping funny stories, but they'd come to an understanding that could only be reached after being at each other's throat.

It was a strange sort of truce between two fighters who each respected the other on some level. Clint respected Jonah as a strong opponent, and the big man respected the speed of Clint's gun hand. Because of that, they were both mounted up and riding east within a few minutes.

Rather than cut the ropes holding Jonah's ankles and legs, Clint made him ride sidesaddle. It wasn't long before that murderous look came back into Jonah's eyes.

Clint did his best not to let the big man catch him smiling.

TWENTY-SIX

They rode for less than two hours before Clint heard the sound of approaching wagon wheels. He'd been getting so tired that he thought the sound was just the wind playing tricks on him again. But soon even his worn-out eyes couldn't miss the sight of movement coming from the trail ahead.

There were two horses escorting a small covered wagon. Clint didn't need to signal them since Jonah started hollering the moment he spotted them. Without changing his pace, Clint steered directly toward the approaching group and waved at them when he was close enough to make out their faces.

He only recognized one of them from earlier in the day. He hadn't caught the man's name, but Clint recalled seeing him at Fischer's side. Besides the two riders, there were two more men driving the wagon. Every one of those men drew his weapon the instant he saw the ropes wrapped around Jonah's arms, legs and torso.

"Well, don't just stand there gawking, assholes," Jonah snarled. "Get me the hell out of this and drop this here son of a bitch!"

Although one of the men swung down from his saddle,

he took his time getting to Jonah's side. It seemed as though he was enjoying the sight of the big man trussed up and riding like a lady and wanted to savor the moment as much as possible. Unable to keep the smirk off his face, the other man drew a blade from a scabbard at his belt and started sawing through the ropes.

Clint was enjoying the sight, but didn't much care for the fact that all the others' guns were still trained on him. "Here," Clint said while reaching into his saddlebag. "Maybe this'll help."

"I wouldn't do that if I was you," said the man sitting next to the wagon driver. He levered a round into his rifle as all the other guns were cocked and made ready.

Clint had been testing the others to get a feel for how they would respond to him. The sound of the hammers being snapped into place raked on his nerves, but he'd heard it too many times to let it unsettle him. Now that he had a feel for the mood of the group, he slowly raised his hand to reveal what he'd been digging for.

Jonah's knife was dangling between Clint's thumb and forefinger. "Just returning this," he said. "Although it's a little worse for wear."

At that moment, the last rope holding Jonah back was cut, and he dropped down from his saddle. The moment his feet hit the dirt, he was storming over to Clint with a stride so fierce it was amazing no steam came from his nostrils.

Jonah closed the distance between him and Clint just as his damaged knife slid from Clint's fingers. The big man swiped his hand out and plucked the knife from the air half a second before it dropped to the ground.

"Thanks for returning this," Jonah said as he took the knife by its handle and lifted the blade up for Clint to see. "Now I can bury it up your ass so far your shit'll come out in slices."

Clint didn't flinch at the other man's sneering gaze or

even at the colorful images he described. His hand did
drift closer to the Colt at his side and was ready to draw
and fire at any possible second.

Staring at Clint's face, savoring the moment for all it
was worth, Jonah had started to pull his arm back for a
solid stab when he was stopped by a sharp voice coming
from behind him.

"Hold it, Jonah," the driver of the wagon said. "That's
not what we're out here for."

"Maybe not. But this is what I'm here for."

"No it isn't. Mr. Fischer said if we caught up with both
of you, we were to tell you to head back to the ranch.
Mr. Adams is a guest now and the order is to treat him
like one."

"A guest?" Jonah said, letting the words dribble from
his mouth like sour milk. "That's bullshit!"

"It don't matter what you think. Those are Mr. Fischer's orders. You want to go against them, that's on
you. Just don't expect anyone to stand behind you if you
go on your own."

Anger flashed on Jonah's face, but most of it still
seemed to be directed at the man directly in front of him.
He glanced back to the wagon as well as to the other men
before stepping back and lowering the blade.

Clint watched this with interest. He would have thought
someone like Jonah would have been just as bent out of
shape by not getting the backup he obviously thought he
deserved. But instead, he didn't hold it against the wagon
driver or anyone else that they weren't about to buck
against their orders. It was obviously well known what
would happen if they did, and it must have been worse
than anything Jonah could offer.

Every step back he took, Jonah appeared to cool off a
little more. Finally he nodded and pointed up at Clint.
"Don't you worry, asshole. Your fight's coming."

Clint nodded right back and said, "I've already had a

go-around with you, big man. I think I know what you're made of. Just drop it right now or you'll only get yourself hurt again."

The others tried to hide it, but it was plain to see that they thought that was pretty amusing. When Jonah looked over at them, they looked away and wiped the grins from their faces real quickly. But Clint saw the smirks and knew that Jonah might have been feared, but was probably not the most popular among Fischer's men.

Still keeping the knife within his clenched fist, Jonah climbed up into his saddle and fixed Clint with one more fierce stare. When he tried to put the knife back into its scabbard, the chipped blade caught on the leather and wouldn't budge. Jonah shoved it down until the steel shredded through leather and wedged into place.

"Sammy's going back with you," the wagon driver said. "Just in case you need help along the way. Them horses look about dead on their feet."

But Jonah was already off and riding away. The young man riding a gray mare next to the wagon pulled away from the others and pointed his horse's nose in the same direction Jonah was headed. "Come on, Mr. Adams," that rider said. "We should be able to make it back before sunrise."

TWENTY-SEVEN

The ride back to Fischer's ranch would have taken much less time if Clint was willing to push Eclipse even further into exhaustion. Since he wasn't about to drive the Darley Arabian to such lengths, he kept a decent pace without pushing too hard.

The younger man that was to escort him back kept in sight and to Clint's left. He didn't strike up any conversations, but Sam was amiable enough whenever Clint had something to say. There didn't seem to be any hostility directed toward him, but that didn't mean Clint was ready to let his guard down.

Whenever he did start talking, Clint asked casual questions or made off handed comments as a way to get a feel for what was truly going on. He decided there was no immediate danger and that the younger man was simply doing the job he'd been told to do. He didn't even seem like the sort to fire a gun at another man. In fact, by the time he could see the ranch house in the distance, Clint was actually beginning to like the kid.

The best part about the long ride back was that Jonah was nowhere to be seen the entire time. Clint had been able to hear the footsteps of a horse in front of him when the ride had first started, but Jonah must have been pushing his animal as hard as it would go. Those sounds got quieter until they disappeared in a matter of minutes.

Clint was certain he'd see the big man when they got to the ranch and wasn't too anxious to speed up the meeting anyway. In fact, if he never saw Jonah again, it would be too soon.

Looking up ahead at the outline of buildings, Clint asked, "Is that the place?"

Sam nodded. "That's the main house. There's smaller ones out back and a few others used for storage and such, but yeah. That's the place."

"It looks pretty impressive."

"It's big, if that's what you mean. I hear it's bigger than some of them plantations down south, but I've never seen one of them."

"Mr. Fischer is a big landowner, I take it."

Sam laughed at that one. Just one short chuckle followed by another nod. "We've been on his land most of the ride. It stretches even farther than this when you head north and west. I'd call that a pretty big landowner."

Whistling softly, Clint sounded as though he was impressed. Not one to be consumed by the need to acquire money or property, Clint respected those that did simply because such men were following through on their own dreams. As far as sheer size and what it would take to truly impress him, Clint had been on Texas ranches that were larger than some small states. Fischer's had a long way to go before it reached those proportions.

The main house itself was very nice indeed. It was two floors high and in very good condition. It was either fairly new or very well maintained. The porch spread across the entire width of the front, which was easily triple the size of most hotels.

As they got closer, Clint could see some of the other buildings Sam had been telling him about. Even those were easy on the eyes and done up to look like smaller versions of the largest structure. Even the barn was constructed and painted to match Fischer's home.

Clint spotted several men on horseback as they got within sight of the house. He couldn't tell for sure that they were armed, but the dozen or so men he saw on foot were displaying their weapons like they were on parade. Each of them had a rifle or shotgun hanging from his hand or propped onto his shoulder.

The presence of an armed patrol made the ranch feel more like a fort than a homestead. Clint couldn't decide yet if those guards were always on patrol or if security had just been stepped up because of what had recently happened so close by. Whichever it was, Clint felt his nerves go on edge when every one of those armed men turned to watch him carefully as he and Sam rode by.

When they finally reached the house, Clint could feel Eclipse's muscles straining beneath him. The stallion had ridden solid for longer than most other horses could handle, but even a champion had its limits. Clint dropped down off the Darley Arabian's back and led him in the rest of the way by the reins.

Sam followed suit and walked as well, mainly because he didn't want to let Clint out of his sight. That much was obvious by the nervous way he glanced over at him from time to time, worrying that Clint was about to do something else he didn't expect.

The kid must have been new to guard duty, Clint thought. Either that or Sam was genuinely concerned with having to deal with someone who'd embarrassed Jonah so badly. Either way, Sam led Clint up to the front door, where a pair of kids no more than nine or ten years old dashed outside to take the reins from both men's hands.

"Don't worry, Mr. Adams," Fischer bellowed as he came striding outside. "Those boys are just going to take the horse to be put up and fed in my stables. I'll even have it brushed and bathed if you like."

Clint handed over Eclipse's reins before the anxious little boy blew a gasket. He said, "Some food, water and rest are all he needs. Thanks all the same, though."

"It's the least I can do. You sure you don't want to treat that stallion to the full service?"

"I'm sure. Besides, I'd hate to get him cleaned off so soon before I have to ride off again."

"You're not planning on staying awhile?" Fischer asked, seeming genuinely disappointed.

"No more than I have to. No offense, but it looks like you've got a lot on your plate right now, and I wouldn't want to impose."

"Nonsense. You get some rest and we can talk about it later. I'll have someone show you to a room, and after you catch a few winks and get some food in your belly, we'll pick this topic up again. Until then, enjoy your stay." And with that, Fischer smiled, turned sharply on his heels and walked back into the house.

Conversation over.

That was fine with Clint since he was too tired to argue anyway.

TWENTY-EIGHT

The inside of the house was as nice as the outside.

That was about all that went through Clint's mind as he was being shown inside and upstairs to a room that was to be his for the time being. All that mattered right then was the fact that the room was quiet and that there was a bed inside. Beyond that, he really didn't care.

A young woman in a simple white dress met him at the front door and took him to just such a room.

"Is this all right, sir?" the young woman asked.

Clint stepped inside and turned to look at her. She was an attractive brunette with delicate features. Her smile was genuine and she made a point not to step over the threshold. "It suits me just fine," Clint replied. "Thank you so much."

She curtsied in a quick, precise motion and kept her smile in place. "If there's anything you need, be sure to ask for me. My name's Daisy and I'll take care of you."

Winking, Clint said, "You'll be the first one I'll ask for just as soon as I get some sleep."

"Make sure that I am." When she said that last sentence, the formality had completely gone from Daisy's voice and she sounded as though she was promising him

112

something more than coffee and biscuits brought up to his room.

Clint kept that in mind, but stored it close to the back. Even if Daisy had stripped down and climbed on top of him, he would have been too tired to enjoy it. After she left he closed the door behind her and took off his hat, jacket and boots. It was reflex to strip down further before climbing into bed, but Clint had to remind himself where he was and what was going on.

He listened at the door for a couple of seconds, until he was certain nobody was directly outside. Glancing around, Clint spotted a chair against the opposite wall which he brought over to the door and wedged under the handle.

The room had a single window, which was large enough for two people to crawl in through. After making sure the latch was in place, Clint hung his jacket from the bottom of the window and set a porcelain water basin on the part of the jacket that touched the floor.

Fischer seemed to be a cordial host, but he'd also had something to do with Jonah coming after Clint the night before. There was no way Clint was about to forget that, which was why he kept most of his clothes along with his gun belt on when he dropped down onto the bed.

He was fairly certain that Fischer wasn't going to kill him in his sleep. Just in case he was wrong about that, Clint trusted his instincts to wake him up if he needed to defend himself. Wanting to stay on the safe side, he sat up on the bed with his back against the headboard. Some raised carving in the wood jammed into his spine, making it just uncomfortable enough to keep him from falling into too deep a sleep.

If someone else came into that room, Clint would know about it. Between the little precautions he'd taken and his own awareness, there wasn't much of anything that could get by him unless it could walk through walls without making a solitary noise.

Clint folded his arms over his chest, settled against the uncomfortable headboard and tilted his head down. His eyelids drooped most of the way down, leaving just enough space for him to see a silver of the room between his lashes. The Colt laid beside him less than a second away from being drawn and fired.

Despite all the wariness and discomfort, Clint still had no problem falling asleep. The entire night and previous day seemed to catch up to him like a piece of lumber knocking into his skull.

Headboard or not, it felt great just to be off his feet. Even though Clint was ready for something to happen at any time, he prayed that it wouldn't. That was the last thing that drifted through his mind before he slipped away into the darkness.

Clint's eyes snapped open and his hand went immediately for his gun. The Colt was there and filled his hand even before he'd leaned forward away from the headboard. There was sunlight coming through his window, but not enough to give him a good idea as to what time it was. Going strictly by the way he felt, Clint figured he might have been asleep for an hour or two.

Swinging his feet over the side of the bed, he looked around the room for any trace of what might have woken him up in the first place. The window hadn't been opened because the jacket was still hanging beneath it and the water basin hadn't been moved. The chair was still wedged beneath the door handle, but when he looked a little closer, Clint noticed there was a bit of space between the edge of the door and the jamb.

Clint got to his feet and moved so that he was standing against the wall next to the door. He worked his way closer to the frame, moving in on the side that was slightly open. Although his hand was still on the Colt's grip, he hadn't drawn the weapon just yet.

That would change real quick depending on who was trying to open the door to his room.

Clint waited until he saw the door start to move again. The motion was barely noticeable, but it still seemed like a quake since he'd been focusing every bit of his attention in anticipation. Whoever was out there was trying the handle again, making sure to keep their efforts as quiet as possible in the process.

Snapping his foot out in a sharp kick, Clint knocked the chair aside and let the door swing open. He was just about to draw the Colt when he got a look at who was standing in the hall. She looked to be in her late twenties and was as attractive as she was shocked by the sudden commotion.

"Did I come at a bad time?" she asked meekly.

TWENTY-NINE

"A bad time?" Clint answered, letting his eyes take in the sight of the woman standing outside his door. "Apart from the fact that I nearly took a shot at you, it's not a bad time at all."

Dark, creamy brown eyes drifted down over Clint's body, stopping at the hand that was still poised over his holstered pistol. "You're not as jumpy as all that," she said. "Can I come in?"

With his heart only just starting to slow down from the way it had been hammering only moments ago, Clint stepped away from the door and allowed the woman to enter. She was dressed in a dark skirt made out of thick cotton. A simple peasant's blouse was beneath a tan, loosely woven shawl that hung over her shoulders. When she walked, the heels of her black leather boots knocked against the floorboards.

"You're Clint Adams?"

"Yes, I am. A very tired one, but Clint Adams all the same."

Extending her hand to him, she said, "I'm Kimberly Fischer. Sorry if I startled you, but I didn't expect the door to be blocked like that."

Clint shook her hand. "You didn't, huh? But you did expect to come walking in here while I was asleep. Mind if I ask what you intended to do once you were inside?"

"That would have depended on if I liked what I saw."

Although that surprised Clint, he did a good job of keeping it from showing on his face. Better to just let it play out on its own, he figured, than try to lead it somewhere else. "Well, you've had your look. Should I turn for you?"

"No need. I like what I see."

"That's just great. Can I get back to sleep now?"

Kimberly smiled and walked over to Clint's bed. The truth of the matter was that he liked what he saw as well. She was trim with tight curves that showed through even beneath the layers of her clothing. Her blouse was the kind that tied in front by laces that ran almost down to her belly. The strings holding the two halves together were loose, allowing Clint to see the upper curve of her firm breasts. As if knowing he was looking at her, she pulled the shawl around her a little tighter, but not before Clint could notice her nipples were hard and poking through the white material.

Kimberly's skin was the color of lightly creamed coffee. That and the shape of her wide, generous mouth made her look either Spanish or possibly Italian. Her hair spilled luxuriously over both shoulders; a cascade of velvety black with streaks of coppery brown. She moved with a grace that couldn't be taught. It was something a woman either did or didn't have and she had it. There was no doubting that.

Keeping his expression stern, Clint said, "I still haven't heard a good reason for you being in here."

"This is my house. I can go where I please."

"Is that how you treat all your guests?"

"Maybe."

"Then my guess is you folks don't have too many get-togethers with anyone but those that are paid to show up."

"You'd be right, Mr. Adams. Or, can I call you Clint?"

"Clint's fine. What should I call you?"

"If you call me over a little closer, you won't be sorry."

Leaving that one hang in the air for a couple moments, Clint still didn't have to wait much longer before Kimberly had stepped up close enough for him to get a breath full of her scent. She smelled like roses and some kind of exotic spice that went straight down to tease something deep inside of him.

"My father said you were coming, but I didn't believe it," she whispered. Now she was close enough for him to feel her breath on his skin when she spoke. "I've heard about you. The Gunsmith. I thought I'd be able to tell if you were really him or not just by looking at you."

"And what's the decision?"

"I'm still not sure yet."

Without warning, Kimberly leaned forward just enough to touch her lips to Clint's. She lingered there for a moment and then kissed him again. The second time still wasn't very long, but she parted her lips just enough to get Clint's lower one between them. She ran her teeth over his lip as though she was tasting him, moaning just loud enough for him to feel the subtle vibration coming from her.

Clint was still running on instinct as his hands came to rest upon her hips, feeling the way she shifted back and forth against him. He could feel the heat of her flesh through all the layers of clothing between them, and soon her hands were caressing him as well.

That second kiss led directly into a third and then a fourth. She would pull back just a little and then kiss him again. Each time was slightly different from the last. Her lips would sometimes merely touch his mouth, or sometimes brush against his neck. Before long, her lips parted to let the tip of her tongue slip into his mouth, sending another jolt of pleasure through his body.

Although Clint hadn't seen that coming, he wasn't about to stop it, either. He let his hands take in the feel of her tight, rounded waist before reaching down to cup the smooth curve of her buttocks. He could hear her moan a little more when he touched her, adding even more heat to their lingering kiss.

Finally, Kimberly moved back. There was only enough distance for her to get a clear look into his eyes, but to Clint it felt like a canyon had just opened up in front of him.

"I've heard some things about Clint Adams," she said. "And they're not the gunfight stories you hear in saloons."

"Really? If you tell me who your source is I'll let you know if I'm worried or not."

She smiled and locked her hands together behind his neck. "It's just a friend of mine who says she met you in Wyoming. After listening to what she had to say, I've been hoping to meet you."

"And are you sure it's really me?"

"Oh yes," she said, reaching down to slide her hand over the bulge between his legs. "I'm sure."

THIRTY

For a minute, Clint thought he had to be dreaming. As he'd been savoring the taste and feel of Kimberly Fischer's lips, he was wondering how that could possibly be the same girl Dave Fischer said was harmed by Mark Tanner. Kimberly wasn't supposed to have been killed or maimed or anything, but after the kind of attack Fischer had described, Clint didn't think she would have been up to the things she was doing now.

When Clint felt her hand stroking him, he knew that he couldn't be dreaming. Her touch was familiar, yet different at the same time. Much like other women who'd touched him there, but still moving with a new rhythm and lingering in spots that even he was surprised to enjoy.

"You like that," she purred. "I can tell. Just like I can tell that you must be the real Gunsmith. I've never heard of a man who could get me so worked up without having to do anything but touch me. That's what she said you were like."

Using the same steely nerve that usually pulled him through a gunfight, Clint got his mind to focus on something else besides the waves of pleasure that Kimberly

was sending through him. "And I was just starting to wonder if you were really Kimberly Fischer."

That seemed to surprise her, but she didn't take her
hand away from him. "And why would you think something like that?"

"Because Mr. Fischer said his daughter was put through
something that would probably make her a little more
cautious around strange men."

"Or maybe a father doesn't need to know about every
little thing that happens in his daughter's bedroom."

"That's true. Except this time, what happened in his
daughter's bedroom might wind up getting another man
killed."

"Who's this you're talking about?"

"Mark Tanner." When he said that name, Clint watched
her carefully. He studied her expression and especially her
eyes, just as though he was sitting across from her at a
poker table. Granted, she wouldn't have been stroking
him in such a familiar way beneath a poker table, but
women had been known to use those same wiles in order
to rake in a pot.

Kimberly's face didn't give a thing away. She still
looked straight into his eyes without once turning away.
And she still looked as though she wanted nothing more
than to feel him on top of her right then and there. "Mark
Tanner was too big a fool to know what he had when he
had it. Besides, he couldn't even handle what I did give
him."

"And what was that?"

"Maybe you should find out for yourself."

Clint was genuinely impressed with how fast Kimberly
managed to get his belt unbuckled and his pants undone.
Before he knew what she'd done, he felt her hand slip
under his clothes so she could take hold of him and stroke
his erect penis.

Although Clint remained confused about her state of

mind, he was still a man and was close to just putting his
questions aside until his more pressing needs were met.
Kimberly's fingers wrapped around his cock and moved
up and down. She smiled at him even wider when she felt
his erection become harder the more she worked it.

"I'd give you so much more than Mark ever had," she
purred. "A man like you could handle everything I've
got."

Clint might have been able to keep himself from throwing Kimberly onto the bed, but he didn't quite have the
strength to push her away entirely. "Now's not the time
for this," he said. But his hands were still roaming over
her buttocks and hips, and she stood with her legs a little
farther apart so he could feel even more of her.

"It's always the time for this," she said, while taking
one of Clint's hands and moving it to the warm spot between her legs. "Can't you feel what a perfect time this
is?"

He felt the heat coming off of her even before his fingers touched her inner thigh through the material of her
skirt. She ground her hips forward, allowing him to probe
even deeper. All he could think of right then was all the
things he wanted to do to her. His mind became even
more distracted when she started whispering all the things
she wanted to do to him.

"I'm here on business," Clint said, more to keep himself on track. He knew that Kimberly wasn't listening to
him. She'd already lowered herself to her knees and
guided his hand to her firm breast. He started to say something else, but his words caught in the back of his throat
before a single one of them got out.

Kimberly was kneeling before him and lowering his
pants just enough to free his penis from his clothes. She
looked at it for a second, lifted her eyes to gaze into his
face and then opened her mouth to take him inside.

THIRTY-ONE

When she wrapped her lips around the tip of his cock, Clint felt a surge of pleasure go through him that was so intense he forgot about everything else that had been on his mind. For a moment, it seemed as though he'd made the long ride and gone through everything else just so he could be right there at that second.

She sucked him just enough for him to feel it as she slid her mouth forward, running her tongue along the bottom of his shaft. Once he was all the way inside, she closed her lips even tighter and then slowly moved her head back again.

Clint had been reaching down to pull her back up to her feet, but instead he threaded his fingers through Kimberly's hair and held the back of her head as she started bobbing back and forth. Her lips and tongue glided over him in an increasing rhythm as she reached out to grab hold of Clint's thighs.

Her eyes were closed now, and she was completely immersed in what she was doing. Kimberly even began making a soft moaning sound in the back of her throat, which sent shivers all the way up to her lips and directly onto Clint's skin.

As soon as she felt him grab hold of her tightly, Kimberly took him all the way into her mouth, kept her lips parted and swirled her tongue around his cock all the way up until she could lick only the tip. She smiled up at him one more time and held her hand out for him to take.

Clint took her hand in his and helped her stand back up. She immediately hiked up her skirt and moved in close so his rigid penis could rub on the bare skin between her legs.

"I want you," she whispered. "I want you to lay me down on that bed and get inside of me."

Just hearing that was enough to make the blood pound even harder in Clint's veins. His hands were roaming on her body and just about every part of him wanted to grant the request she'd just made. But there was one part that made him stop: his gut instinct.

Unfortunately, he was used to listening to that part above all others.

Clint moved his hands down below their waists until he could feel the silky skin of her inner thigh. The edge of his thumb grazed along the soft thatch of hair between her legs and lingered there for about a second before moving on. When he reached down to pull his own pants up and fasten them, he saw a look of genuine surprise come across Kimberly's face.

"We'll pick up with this soon," he said. "Real soon. But right now, there's other matters I need to check on."

She stepped away and let her skirt drop down to cover her. "We'll see about that. Maybe I won't feel like picking this up again."

"Maybe. But something tells me you will." With that, Clint reached out to put one arm around Kimberly's shoulders so he could pull her in close. He planted a kiss on her that contained all the passion and desire that had been building up inside of him from the moment he'd first felt her hands on his body.

Kimberly tried to pull away, but only for a moment. Soon, she melted into his embrace and moaned quietly as he brushed his tongue against her lips one at a time. She was nearly out of breath by the time he was finished with that single kiss and did her best to look slightly offended when he let her go.

"When will I see you again?" he asked.

"Maybe never, Mr. Adams. If you're lucky, I won't tell my father about this."

"If I'm lucky, you'll find me later tonight."

Already walking toward the door, Kimberly paused and glanced over her shoulder. Touching a hand to her lips which were still warm from Clint's touch, she said, "We'll just see about that."

Turning her head so quickly that her hair was flung out to one side, Kimberly pulled open the door and huffed through it. When she shut it behind her, it seemed as though she was about to slam it but changed her mind at the last second. She just closed it instead and her feet made a quick pattering sound as she moved down the hall.

Now that he was alone, Clint could let out the breath he'd been holding and drop the mask of calmness that had been getting harder to maintain with each second that passed. No matter how much of what was happening seemed odd or out of place, that didn't make it any easier for him to turn away a beautiful woman. Add to it the amazing talents Kimberly had just demonstrated and the task became even more difficult.

Clint's brain told him that Kimberly Fischer should not be acting anything like that if her father had been telling him the truth. Beyond that, there was something about the speed and insistence in her manner that made Clint feel she was trying to get him distracted instead of just into bed.

Perhaps he was just getting too suspicious in his old age. Women could be just as forward as men behind closed doors. Anyone who thought different probably hadn't been around too many women. But Kimberly was something besides merely aggressive. Clint couldn't quite figure out what the problem was, but every instinct in him said that he needed to tread lightly around anyone remotely connected to the Fischers.

Well, almost every instinct.

The rest of Clint's body and soul was still thinking about how good Kimberly's hands and lips had felt on him. And it would be that part of him that would keep thinking about what she'd done to him until he was able to return the favor. He was already about to kick himself for not indulging himself just a little bit longer while she was still there.

Her scent still lingered in the air as if to taunt him even more. If anyone else had told him about doing what he'd just done, he would have laughed and called him a fool.

But that didn't matter anymore. There was business he needed to see to and things that needed to be done. Besides, Clint was certain he hadn't seen the last of Kimberly Fischer. One way or another, she'd be back soon.

All the same, he stepped over to the basin in the corner of his room, dipped his hands in the cool water and splashed some on his face. It took a few more splashes to take the edge off the fire Kimberly had started inside of him. It wasn't enough to cool him off completely, but at least Clint could focus on something else besides the smoothness of her skin and the way she moved her mouth slowly over him.

Actually, a few more splashes couldn't hurt.

THIRTY-TWO

Although he was still a little hot under the collar, Clint was no longer about to collapse from exhaustion. Between the bit of sleep he'd gotten, Kimberly's wake-up call and the cold water afterward, Clint was actually awake and alert by the time he opened his door and stepped out into the hall.

His was third in a row of doors that stretched down toward the stairs before turning into a corner which wrapped around the other side of the building. The hall-way stretched out for a ways in the other direction as well, making the upper floor of the ranch house a rectangular path which led to at least ten different rooms. There might have been more, but Clint wasn't about to start wandering around on an unguided tour.

Heading toward the stairs, he backtracked along the same path that he'd been shown to get to his room. There were plenty of footsteps and voices coming from various rooms and the floor below, so he had no doubt he'd be stumbling upon someone fairly soon.

When Clint made it to the head of the stairs, he looked down with one foot poised and ready to take that first step. Looking back up at him was Dave Fischer himself, in much the same position at the bottom of the staircase.

"Why, Mr. Adams. I was just about to come and see if you were doing all right in your room," Fischer said. "Actually, I didn't think you'd be awake."

"Well, I'm sure that wouldn't have stopped you. The lock on my door doesn't seem to function too well." Despite the sharp tone in his voice, Clint managed to keep his smile intact. The mixed signals put a somewhat bewildered look upon the silver-haired man's face.

Fischer shook off that expression and immediately put on another more familiar one. It was the same stern gaze that he'd shown to all his men, but mixed in with a softer undertone. Of course, the sternness was the only part of him that seemed completely genuine.

"Was there some kind of trouble that I don't know about?" Fischer asked.

"Not at all. Everything got straightened out eventually."

"Glad to hear it. Like I said, I was about to come check on you and leave you this." Raising his left hand, Fischer displayed a folded piece of paper that he was holding. "It's an invitation to dinner, but I can relay the message to you in person. Are you certain you wouldn't like to lay down for a little while longer? You can't be fully rested after all that riding."

"Dinner?" Digging into his pocket, Clint pulled out a watch that he'd bought not too long ago and flipped open the cover. It was three-thirty in the afternoon. A bit late to be getting out of bed, but not so much so considering that he'd only been asleep for six hours or so.

Clint had to double-check the watch in his hand. No wonder he seemed so rested. Looking back on it, he swore he hadn't even fully closed his eyes after getting situated on his bed. Even knowing that he'd fallen asleep at some point, Clint would have sworn even harder that he hadn't been out for more than two hours at the most.

"Something wrong, Mr. Adams?"

"No. I just lost track of the time, is all. When is dinner?"

"Six o'clock, but I imagine you must be awfully hungry right now. I can arrange for my cook to fix you something if you'd like."

"That sounds great," Clint said as he started walking down the stairs. It was obvious that Fischer wasn't about to climb up to meet him, and the silver-haired man even seemed to be getting impatient with having to lift his chin for so long without an apology. "I was actually hoping to find you."

"Really? I was just about to make my daily rounds. Perhaps you'd like to join me?"

"I'd like that."

Fischer turned sharply on the balls of his feet and began walking away from the stairs using long, powerful strides. "Then come this way," he said while motioning for Clint to follow him. "I've got a lot on my plate right now, but I can talk and ride at the same time. That'll give the cook enough time to throw something together for you and have it ready by the time we get back."

Snapping his fingers to the first person he spotted along the way, Fischer barked out a series of orders to be relayed to the cook. The person on the receiving end of the commands was a young girl who was still new to her teens. She paid rapt attention to everything Fischer said, nodded and curtsied when he was finished, and then dashed off toward the kitchen.

Fischer had already moved on. He struck Clint as the type who never stayed around to see if anyone heard what he'd said just because he'd much rather yell at them about it later. The silver-haired man didn't say much else to Clint until they'd cut directly through the middle of the house and come out on the opposite side.

The back door opened onto a large porch which was identical to the one spanning the front of the building.

Still walking as though he was being pulled by a freight train, Fischer headed straight for a livery that was less than twenty paces away.

"They should be finished with your horse by now, Mr. Adams. I'll have someone bring him around and help you with the saddle."

"Actually," Clint said. "I'd rather let him rest awhile longer. Is there another one I could use instead?"

Laughing as though Clint had just told him a slightly amusing joke, Fischer nodded. "I've got more horses than a breeder, Mr. Adams. I'll have one of them prepared along with mine."

Clint was getting tired of hearing Fischer say "Mr. Adams" so many times during their conversation. It wasn't so much the words as the snide, almost condescending way the other man said them. Clint would have tried to correct it, but something told him that Fischer would just find another way to get under his skin.

It was better to deal with a familiar problem than ask for a new one. Clint had plenty to make him feel uneasy already, and the longer he stayed around men like Dave Fischer and Mark Tanner, the more that uneasiness just seemed to multiply.

THIRTY-THREE

The horse provided to Clint was a fine animal by anyone's standards. Of course, riding with Eclipse for so long had raised Clint's standards considerably, and he noticed the difference in the other animal right away. It was a brown and white gelding that responded well to Clint's commands and seemed eager enough to head out for a run.

Knowing that Eclipse had that much more time to rest up after all the work he'd done was enough to make Clint happy to ride a pack mule if he needed. Fischer was on a different mount as well, only his was taller and much more muscled than the one riding next to him. Clint was certain this was completely on purpose.

"I've sent out another two groups of men to track down that skunk," Fischer said. "Between them all, I figure I'll be looking into that bastard's eyes before dawn tomorrow. I just need to make sure that there aren't any holes in my security just in case that son of a bitch decides to double back and finish what he started."

"And what might that be?"

Fischer's eyes snapped over to look at Clint as though he'd forgotten the other man was there. That expression only lasted a split second before it was replaced by the man's usual stern mask. "He's got something against my family, Mr. Adams. I told you that already."

"From what you told me, it sounded like he'd done his damage and was trying to get away with his life. That is, unless you haven't told me everything yet."

Having ridden away from the stables, Fischer was making a straight line toward the edge of his property. The men he passed tipped their hats or waved to him, but the older man didn't gesture in return. Instead, he simply glanced in their direction like a general on inspection detail. After mulling over his thoughts for a little bit, Fischer turned just enough to let Clint know that he was addressing him and not the open air.

"You ever owned property before, Mr. Adams?"

Somehow, the silver-haired man seemed to catch on to the way Clint bristled whenever he heard his name spoken that way. As expected, Fischer was adding even more emphasis to just the right syllables so it grated on Clint's nerves even more.

"No, Dave," Clint answered, addressing the other man in a way he was sure would elicit a similar response. "I move around too much to be tied down to a piece of land."

Fischer nodded and smirked slightly, but it was plain to see that he didn't like being addressed in such a common manner. "Well, when a man owns his land, there's always someone out to take it from him. That's a hard and cold fact of life, Mr. Adams. People are hurtful by nature and will take whatever they can get if they think they can get it."

"You don't need to be a landowner to know that," Clint said. "I'm quite familiar with cold, hard facts like that."

"Maybe so. And you did see what was done to my family and workers who were unfortunate enough to be on that wagon?"

"Yes, I did."

"Then you know who I'm dealing with."

"That's just the thing," Clint said, his interest in the conversation suddenly perking up again. "I thought I knew who I was dealing with until I ran into some trouble after the last time we parted ways."

"Trouble?"

"Don't look all surprised, Dave. Jonah works for you. I don't see him as the type to have many original thoughts, so that means he was doing what you told him to do."

Fischer's face brightened slightly, as though he'd only then recalled a man named Jonah on his payroll. "Ah yes. There was some trouble, wasn't there? I was hoping you weren't about to make me broach the subject."

"I'll gladly broach it. How about I start off by asking why the hell you would send someone to knock my head off when all I did was agree to help you and your men?"

After rounding a tree with a trunk wider than several grown men's arm spans, Fischer turned north and headed toward a group of men riding toward him. "That's not exactly the way Jonah described it."

"I'll bet it isn't. Last time I saw him, he was scampering off after trying again to gut me with that blade he likes so damn much."

"Come now, Mr. Adams. Are you going to tell me that you didn't knock Jonah unconscious, leave him in the open and then strap him onto his own horse? My men came back saying that they found you pulling Jonah behind you and he looked beaten within an inch of his life."

"You might need spectacles, then," Clint said. "Because you must not have taken a real good look at me. I'm not exactly how I was the last time you saw me and this is after some time to rest and wash up a bit."

"Granted."

"Whatever Jonah told you, he must know that he's damn lucky to be alive. I did leave him tied up for a bit, but that was just to keep him away from me while I did some searching for a killer. And believe me when I tell you it would have been a whole lot easier to shoot him instead of dragging his ass back to where your men would find him."

That hung in the air for a couple seconds as Fischer turned his eyes toward the guards patrolling his perimeter. The muscles in his jaw tensed as though he was physically chewing on something, until he finally let out a short huff of air. "All right. Jonah might have gotten a little overly anxious. He tends to do that sometimes."

"Really? And what was he supposed to do when you sent him back for me?"

"Keep an eye on you. If you got out of line, he was to make sure you quickly saw the error of your ways."

"Well, I was followed and then attacked. That's a long way from being overly anxious."

"If discipline is what you're asking about, Mr. Adams, you can rest assured that Jonah is regretting what he did. If you want more than that, I'm afraid I just don't have the time. Your help would still be appreciated, but I don't intend on going back and forth with you about matters that are already over and done with."

Clint let out a short, humorless laugh. "I'll agree with you on that, but it seems like I still haven't gotten an answer to my question. Why send him after me?"

"Because I know that that killer was working with others and I needed to be sure you weren't one of them."

"Now we're getting somewhere," Clint said. "Now tell me about how you know Mark Tanner."

"He worked for me as a driver for one of my wagons until he started getting the idea of using what he'd learned from me and going into business on his own."

"And you couldn't allow that, right?"

Fischer glanced over at him and shook his head once. "No, Mr. Adams. I couldn't."

"Why not just fire him and be done with it?"

"He knows too much."

"About what?"

Fischer didn't answer right away. He paused just then and got a look for a fleeting moment as though he'd been struck in the face. It didn't last long, but it was the most informative thing Clint had gotten since he'd started this dance of words with him.

THIRTY-FOUR

In poker, it was known as a tell. Some men scratched their noses when they had a good hand and some played with their chips when they thought they were going to lose. Those things were all tells, and being able to spot them was what separated a good card player from a poor one.

Clint knew that brief look and subtle twitch was one of Fischer's tells, and spotting that was a major victory. He wasn't sure exactly what, but Clint knew that something had struck a nerve within Fischer regarding something Mark Tanner learned or had stolen from him. Just the fact that he was hiding something regarding that subject was enough to pique Clint's interest.

Any man who'd been visited by a thief was usually more than open about what had been taken from him. After all, that was the way those things were found and returned. Most folks would have no trouble returning stolen property as long as they knew what it was. All in all, people did like to help when they could.

If something bothered him about whatever it was that Tanner had, that meant Fischer had a reason to hide that information. Either he was missing something he shouldn't have had in the first place or it was something that he wasn't too proud of owning. Whichever it was, it meant that Fischer was hiding something.

As much as Clint blamed his circumstances or standing as the cause for landing him in so many sticky situations, his curiosity was just as often the true culprit. If he needed proof of that, all he had to do was focus on the itch that formed in the back of his head once he knew that the old man was guarding some kind of dirty secret.

Normally, Clint would have been more than happy to let him have his secret and be on his way. Lord knows he had plenty of secrets of his own. But once keeping that secret had caused Fischer to put others in harm's way, Clint figured he was obliged to bring it out into the light of day.

It was times like that when he felt even more bound by that singular law he would honor above all others. And if that law allowed him to indulge his curiosity, then that was just a fringe benefit. Besides, Clint couldn't think of a better way to wipe that smug look off of Dave Fischer's face.

"What Tanner stole from me isn't important," Fischer said as all those thoughts blazed through Clint's mind. "What is important is that he's found because once he's found, I'll have what I need. Your help would be appreciated, but it's not necessary, Mr. Adams. The train he got started will keep rolling with or without you. Make no mistake about that."

Clint didn't have to give a reply to that, and it didn't look as though Fischer was expecting one. By that point, Clint already knew things were too far gone to be stopped without some kind of crash at the end. He was there, and it was his duty to make sure that the crash took the right people down with it.

Nobody had given him that duty but himself. If capable men couldn't lend their skills where they were needed, then there wasn't much hope in the world. That was the only law. And now more than ever, it was getting pounded into his head that he needed to abide by it.

"So what's it going to be?" Fischer said. "If you'd rather not have a part in this due to an unfortunate transgression by one of my employees, that's your choice. You can stay for your meal or even another night, and I'll make sure you have enough supplies to be on your way. No hard feelings.

"If, however, you would accept my apology and help me in this matter of apprehending a dangerous criminal, you will have my assurance that Jonah will not be allowed to make another mistake. In fact, I'm certain he very much regrets what happened already."

Clint nodded at that, noticing that Fischer said the big man regretted what happened. Not what he did. Most men would rather twist the truth or play with words than outright lie. Lying was a skill and was best left to the professionals. Jonah was probably getting another beating handed to him for not doing whatever Fischer had really ordered him to do once he'd found his target.

That was just another thing pushing Clint toward the decision he knew he was going to make anyway. "I'll stay," he told the silver-haired man riding beside him. "I want to help work this situation out and make sure this back-stabbing cheat gets what's coming to him."

"Excellent, Mr. Adams. I'm sure you won't regret this."

Clint returned the other man's smile, marveling at the way Fischer couldn't tell when his own word plays were being turned and pointed back at him. Clint never said exactly who he thought the back-stabbing cheat was. All he said was that he would get what's coming to him.

That last sentiment was as true as gospel.

THIRTY-FIVE

As he'd been following Fischer on his inspection tour of the ranch, Clint had been making a subtle inspection of his own. He'd been keeping his eyes open and noting all the men that Fischer nodded to, observing how the men were armed and paying attention to any gut reactions he might have had regarding what kind of men they were.

Clint's instincts were good, but he was no mind reader. The impression he got was that Fischer's men were mostly thugs who enjoyed carrying guns but didn't really use them that often. A few of the men looked nervous, as though they'd been forced to take their weapon along with them. A few of them also looked like they might be a genuine threat if the lead started to fly.

Of the ones he'd seen, Clint remembered four faces to watch out for in the time to come. He counted twenty-two men in all, spread across the property in groups of three or four. Although that could add up to trouble if Fischer turned all those men against him, for one very good reason Clint was happy to see so many hands out and about. If they were patrolling the ranch, that meant they couldn't be watching the house.

After agreeing to stay on for a bit, Clint excused himself so he could head back to the house and fill his grumbling belly. His first stop was to the livery so he could drop off his borrowed horse. While he was there, he made sure to pay Eclipse a visit just to make sure the stallion was being well cared for.

Eclipse had already been brushed and fed. The familiar spark was in the Darley Arabian's eyes and he even looked at Clint as though he was anxious to get moving. Patting the horse's neck, Clint looked around at the layout of the stable. He spotted a few doors and committed the layout to memory. He wasn't completely certain he was going to make a hasty exit, but it never hurt to be prepared.

Tossing a silver dollar to the livery boy, Clint left the stable and walked back to the house. Fischer had been good as his word, and a hot meal was waiting for him as soon as he walked through the back door. One of the housekeepers greeted him and swept him to a dining room, where he was served a ham steak, biscuits and potatoes.

The food was great and made Clint feel better than he had in a while. Between the lack of sleep and the hard riding, he'd been starting to feel the strain that had been put on him in the last day or two. It wasn't anything that was about to kill him, but he sure noticed when that strain was lifted.

"Is there anything else I can get for you?" one of the young servants asked. She was a cute little girl wearing a black and white dress. Brown hair was pulled back into a long tail that curled at the end toward the middle of her back.

Clint smiled and patted his stomach. "I couldn't stuff in another bite. Mr. Fischer said I should just make myself at home and rest up before I head out again."

"If you need anything, I can get it for you."

"No thanks, sweetie. I'll just wander around here and take a look at this nice house."

The girl looked a little uncertain, but Clint put just the right amount of authority in his voice and mixed it with a kind tone which put the girl's mind at ease. She cleared away the dishes and hurried off to the kitchen, where an older woman was cleaning things up.

Clint walked out of the dining room and walked straight for the staircase which led up to his bedroom. With Mr. Fischer out of the house, the workers there were much more relaxed and went about their chores without paying too much attention to their guest. Clint did get a few glances, but he pretended not to notice and they went away as long as he kept moving in the proper direction.

The instant he saw that there was nobody around, Clint took a sharp detour and turned away from the staircase. There were more rooms beyond the stairs and he headed for those instead of going up to the second floor.

Since the half of the house he'd seen so far appeared to be devoted mostly to casual things such as dining, sitting or entertaining, he headed for the other half. Clint hoped there was something he could find that might shed some light on what was going on. He didn't know exactly what he was looking for, but he was certain he'd know it when he found it.

Almost immediately, the house became more enclosed than the rest of what he'd seen. More curtains were drawn and more shutters were closed. He passed more closed doors as well as he walked through a hallway that was considerably more cramped than the open airiness of the more public areas of the house.

For that reason, he had to backtrack slightly until he got to a lantern sitting on an end table near the staircase. He snagged the lantern when none of the servants were nearby and lit it as he made his way back to the other side of the house.

Walking with the lantern in hand, as he started trying to open doors and peek inside Clint was reminded of the cave where Mark Tanner had been hiding. The closed-in rooms were dark and quiet as that cave, except Clint was feeling even more uneasy as he stepped inside of them.

At least he knew what he was looking at inside a cave and couldn't be so easily locked inside. The closed-off rooms of Fischer's house felt as though they hadn't been opened in some time. In fact, Clint felt a chill run down his spine which was similar to the feeling he got when walking through the home of someone who was no longer among the living.

Most of those rooms were nothing special. Mainly sitting rooms, a parlor and some storage so far. But the air inside those places felt dead and hung behind the doors like thick smoke. Even his footsteps seemed to echo more within those rooms, making Clint instinctively feel like he needed to get out and back to someplace where there were more people about.

The next door Clint opened led to what appeared to be a study. At first when he'd tried to open it, the handle didn't budge. Thinking it was locked, Clint was about to move on when the handle clanked and then the door swung open.

He looked around and immediately noticed the desk in the middle of the room, surrounded by bookcases on three sides. There was a fireplace on the outer wall which was filled with a layer of soot and covered by an ornamental iron grate. A burgundy carpet covered most of the floor, muffling the sounds which would have echoed in all the other rooms Clint had seen.

There were no windows in that room, but still it managed to seem less like a tomb than the others where the windows had been almost completely covered. Clint looked around at the rest of the walls and spotted something that had gotten past him in all the other rooms he'd checked so far.

Maybe it was because the lighting was different due to the lack of windows. What little illumination there was filtered in through the open door and was only slightly helped along by the flickering light of the lantern in Clint's hand. The walls were completely bare, except in that different light, he could tell that they hadn't always been that way. There were shapes spaced along the walls that were a little cleaner than the rest. Some were rectangles, but most were squares of varying sizes, all placed at eye level.

Picture frames.

That had to have been what were hanging on the walls, except someone had taken them all down.

Clint wondered why someone would do that. Moving in to take a closer look, he pushed the door shut behind him so his light wouldn't be seen. He was only able to get the door partly closed before it was stopped. Just as he was turning to look at what was blocking the door, he heard a voice behind him.

"You shouldn't be in here."

THIRTY-SIX

When Clint spun around to look at who had just asked him that question, his muscles tensed, but he didn't make a move toward his gun. Part of that was because he was getting used to being on edge over the last day or two, but mostly it was because of the meekness soaked into the light, wavering voice.

The one who'd spoken was a girl with light brown hair who looked like she couldn't have weighed a hundred pounds soaking wet. Her skin was smooth and tanned and her eyes were wide and alert. The first thing that struck Clint was how familiar she looked. Then he realized she resembled the little girl who'd cleared away his breakfast dishes if she'd been sped through the next five or six years.

"It's all right," Clint said, easing back and putting on a comforting smile. "I'm not going to hurt you."

The girl took a step back and stopped. That was when Clint noticed she wasn't wearing any shoes and padded over the floor without making a sound. At least that explained how she'd managed to get the drop on him.

"You're real quiet," Clint said, not mentioning the part where her silent steps had almost earned her a bigger scare

than she'd already gotten. "Sorry if I seemed cross just
now."

Her shoulders lowered from around her ears and a good
deal of the fright disappeared from her face. "I didn't
mean to scare you," she said. "But you really shouldn't
ought to be here."

"I'm a guest of Mr. Fischer. My name is Clint. What's
yours?"

"Grace."

"That's a pretty name."

Now that she wasn't so scared of him, the girl straightened her posture and looked him in the eye. She appeared
to be somewhere in her early teens and already showed
the potential to become a real heartbreaker. "My little sister said you were headed this way when you should have
gone upstairs. You're not supposed to come in here. Nobody is."

"What about Mr. Fischer?" Clint asked. "Doesn't he
come in here?"

"No. Not anymore."

"Why not?"

She paused for a second and looked around at the study.
Clint noticed the sadness creep into her eyes as if she,
too, was looking at the room of someone dearly departed.
"If you don't come out of here, I'll get in trouble. Nobody's supposed to be in here and if anyone finds out . . ."

Letting a bit of guilt show on his own face, Clint said,
"Don't worry. If anyone finds out, I'll probably be in
worse trouble than you." From there, he stepped farther
inside the room and walked up to the desk. "Whose is
this?"

"Mr. Fischer's," Grace answered in a hurried whisper.
"Now get out of there."

"And whose things are these?" Clint asked as he slowly
opened one of the desk drawers and began poking around
inside.

That brought Grace rushing into the room, just as Clint had planned. Even in her haste, the girl's feet made as much noise as a heavy cat padding over the floorboards. "Don't look in there! You'll get us both in a fix if we don't get out of here right now."

Once she was beside the desk, Clint shut the drawer. It had been empty anyway, but apparently Grace didn't know that. He could see that she was afraid of something besides him now and was desperate to get him out of there. That, more than anything, told him that he was close to finding something very important.

"Where are the pictures, Grace?"

The girl froze for a moment and then took a step back. "Huh? What pictures?"

Clint walked to the closest square spot on the wall and pointed to it. "The picture that had been hanging right here," he said. "And there and all over the room. You can tell there were pictures hanging there. Where are they now?"

"I don't know."

"Do you know why someone would want to hide them?"

Grace was quiet and looked away from him. Her hands knotted together, and she pressed her knuckles beneath her chin.

"You're going to be a heartbreaker," Clint said as he gently lifted her head up with a finger beneath her chin. "But you'll never be any good at poker."

Even though she clearly didn't understand his reference, Grace knew that she couldn't lie to him. The longer she stared up into Clint's face, however, the more she seemed to convince herself that he wasn't about to hurt her.

"You said this is Mr. Fischer's office," Clint said. "But it's obvious nobody's been in here for a while. I don't think anyone's been in most of the rooms in this wing for some time. Why is that?"

"Because," Grace said. She strained with the thoughts that were obviously running through her head. It was plain to see that she knew what she wanted to say, but she just couldn't get the words out.

"Mr. Fischer is hiding something, isn't he?" Clint offered as a way to guide the girl in the proper direction. He was getting an uneasy feeling in his gut, as though some watch in his mind had ticked too many times. He didn't have much time before someone else found him there. He needed to speed things up, but had to be careful not to scare away the girl. "Does it have something to do with Mark Tanner?"

Grace shook her head.

"Then what about Mr. Fischer?" Clint asked, repeating the name that had brought about the most reaction in the girl's face. "He seems like he might get mad at you or the rest of the people working for him. Or what about his daughter?"

Suddenly, Grace was unable to look at him any longer. She turned her face away and pressed her hands against her eyes. Her shoulders started to shake and the sobs that emerged from her racked her entire body.

Clint started to reach out to comfort her, but Grace pulled away from him and ran across the room. Clint thought she was about to bolt from the room, but instead she turned and ran for a smaller door on the wall adjacent to the fireplace.

She pulled open that door, ran inside and disappeared. The sounds of her crying could still be heard, reminding Clint even more of the haunted feeling he'd gotten when searching through the study earlier. Walking over to look inside what he could tell was a closet, he stopped when he saw Grace come out again.

The girl looked small and frightened. Her arms were

clasped in front of her as though she was trying to embrace herself, but then Clint noticed she was actually embracing something else. That something was rectangular in shape and narrow enough for Grace to wrap her arms completely around it.

"Here," she said, walking up to Clint and loosening her arms so he could see what she'd been embracing.

The object she was offering to him was a picture frame. Clint took it from her and turned it around so he could see the photograph of a man with dark hair surrounded by three other people. One of them was a woman with long, lighter colored hair who seemed happy even after standing next to him for all the time it had taken to take the picture. The others were slightly younger visions of Grace and her little sister.

"This is Mr. Fischer," Grace said in a voice that was full of certainty. "And that lady that was in your room isn't his daughter. Me and my sister are his daughters. Nobody else."

THIRTY-SEVEN

For a moment, Clint could only stare down at the picture in that girl's hands. As he did, he felt the pieces he'd been looking for not only revealing themselves to him but fitting into place as well. He was a long way from knowing everything that had been going on in that house, but at least now he was pointed in the right direction.

"Are the rest of the pictures in there?" he asked.

Grace nodded and walked back into the closet.

Following the girl, Clint stepped through the door and brought the lantern with him. He couldn't go much farther simply because the closet was barely big enough for Grace to walk inside. He looked around within the cramped little space and saw it was packed with stacks of items that had been thrown in there as though whoever had done it never wanted to see them again. There wasn't one neat pile, but there sure was a whole lot of broken glass and broken possessions.

Grace was crouching in the only place she could: an empty patch of floor that wasn't much bigger around than she was. When she stood up, she was clutching a stack of frames and papers to her chest as if she was afraid to let them go. Reluctantly, she loosened her grip and handed them over to Clint.

There were only three more frames in the pile Clint was given. Those were cracked and coming apart, and when he glanced at the spot where Grace had been looking, he quickly spotted the remains of the other frames lying in ruins upon the floor.

The picture on top of the stack he was holding was a loose photograph of the man and woman from the first picture. They had been photographed with her seated and him standing behind her. Their expressions were stern and their bodies were posed, which told Clint the picture had most likely been taken at a studio.

The next picture was of the two girls. They were also posed and standing in front of the same fancy backdrop that had been used in the previous picture. Both girls were wearing their Sunday best and seemed bored to tears.

Clint flipped through the rest of the photos until he got to the three that were still in frames. All of them were various family portraits, most of which featured the man and his family. The ones in frames were older and probably of grandparents or some other more distant relatives.

"That's my family," Grace said. "That's Mr. and Mrs. Fischer. My parents."

After flipping through the entire stack of photos, Clint had to come back to the one that was on top to begin with. He looked at the couple and felt connected to them in a strange kind of way. It was something he felt when he looked at a lot of photographs. Seeing their faces frozen in that moment in time made him wonder about what the subjects were thinking about and if some of that was still reflected in their eyes.

Looking at the face of that man in the picture, Clint had no trouble at all imagining him in the very study where he was standing just then. He could picture a fire roaring and the bookshelves free of dust. Clint could even picture that man sitting behind his desk, going over the paperwork that came with owning land.

"What happened to them, Grace?" he asked. Suddenly, Clint felt bad for putting the question so bluntly, since he knew it would upset the girl. But time was running out and whatever hurt Grace was feeling, Clint doubted he could make it much worse.

"He's gone," she said in a voice that reminded Clint more of the little girl from one of the more faded pictures in his hand. "He's gone and so is my mother."

"Who is Dav—" Clint stopped himself before he called the man who was in charge of the ranch by the wrong name. After handing the pictures back, Clint waited for Grace to stack the photos and frames back exactly where she'd found them.

When she was done with that task, Clint took Grace by the hand and led her toward the desk. There was a chair against the wall and he took her to it. She didn't want to touch anything else around her, however, so Clint set the lantern down on the edge of the desk. "Who are all these people living here now?" he asked after taking a quick look out the door. "What happened to your family?"

Grace clutched her arms around herself as though she could still feel those picture frames in her grasp. When she glanced around at the lonely remains of her father's study, she seemed to find a renewed source of strength. She looked into Clint's eyes and spoke in a quiet, yet fierce voice.

"I don't know who these people are," she told him. "Not really. They came here about a month ago. My father said there were some men trying to steal our supplies and make off with the horses. He and some of the others went out to find them and chase them off."

"Did anyone ever call the sheriff?"

"Poppa said the sheriff was too far away and that we

had to take care of things on our own. At least, that's
what he told Mother."

Some of the sadness was creeping back into her voice,
replacing the determination that had been there moments
ago. Before she lost her strength, Clint took hold of her
by the shoulders and made her look him in the eyes again.

"I'm here to help you," he said. "But I can only do that
if I know what's going on here. I know it's hard for you,
but you're the best chance I've got of finding out the truth.
Can you tell me what you know so I can help you?"

Grace started to answer several times, but choked on
her words each time. Finally, she took a deep breath and
nodded once. "I'll help you, but not here. They'll be looking for me if I'm gone too long."

Suddenly, Clint felt a stab of panic in his stomach.
"Does everyone know who you are?"

"Just get out of here and meet me in the pantry. It's a
little door in the back of the kitchen. I'll tell the others
you're coming."

Clint wanted to get everything out in the open right
then and there. He'd been waiting so long to hear what
Grace knew that the thought of being found sounded almost worth the risk. But the girl had already left him alone
in the study. Her padded footsteps quickly faded away to
dead quiet.

THIRTY-EIGHT

Clint took his lantern and left the study. The latch on the door was obviously broken, but he managed to close the door solidly enough that it wasn't immediately noticeable. Just to be sure he gave the girl enough time to make her preparations, he made his way slowly down the rest of the hall, glancing into the rooms when he could and testing the door handles when he couldn't.

All the while, he expected someone else to come around the corner and discover him making his rounds. By that time, he was hoping to be found just so he didn't have to worry about the possibility hanging over his head like a hammer. But even though he heard heavy steps coming from the other part of the house, as well as thumping up and down the stairs, none of those people seemed interested in going down Clint's hall.

The walkway led all the way around to the back of the house, ending in a large sunroom filled with empty ceramic pots and abandoned wicker chairs. It was a very peaceful room, or at least it must have been when it was full of light and plants. Even though all the light couldn't be kept out of the room, the drawn curtains filtered out just enough to make the place seem more shady than in-

viting. Clint's steps echoed through the room and he was
more than happy to turn around and head back out again.

It had been a couple minutes since he'd left Grace and
he figured it would take a couple more for him to work
his way back to the kitchen. As he moved down the hall-
way retracing his steps, Clint was especially alert for
someone coming around the next corner. That uneasy
feeling in his gut told him that his time alone was up and
that someone would be looking for him at any moment.

He made it all the way to the staircase before he heard
soft footsteps making their way from the upper floor. Clint
extinguished the lantern, set it down where he'd found it
and walked toward the front door.

"There you are," came a familiar voice from a little
ways up the staircase. "I've been looking for you."

Clint turned and smiled. He'd recognized Kimberly's
voice after the first word. "I was just about to head outside
to walk off my breakfast."

"Did you get a little lost?"

"Just a little. I thought I might catch up with Mr. Fischer or at least find someone to tell me when he'll be
back."

"Did you find anyone?"

"Not yet. Care to help me out?"

Looking at him as though she wasn't sure if she was
going to believe him or not, Kimberly moved down the
rest of the stairs until she was standing at Clint's side.
"When my father wants to meet up with you, he'll find
you. Until then, I'd like to have some time with you myself. I thought you'd be in your room, but I'm glad I
didn't have to look too far for you."

"Actually, I need to get back out and follow up on a
trail I found the other day. If you could tell your father
I'm leaving, I'd really appreciate it."

Kimberly lowered her head slightly and let her bottom
lip droop in a pout that was both sad and attractive at the

same time. "You don't want to pick up where we left off?"

Moving in so that their bodies were almost touching, Clint lowered his voice to a whisper. "You know I do, but I also want to find that bastard that hurt you and those people. What about tonight?"

"What about it?"

"Come find me and we can see what happens."

"And what if I don't feel like trailing after you?"

"Then I'll find you." Punctuating his statement with a grazing touch along her side, Clint let his eyes stay on hers just long enough for the tension to build before he winked and walked out the front door. Before he shut the door behind him, he could feel Kimberly's eyes on his back as though there was heat radiating from her.

Now that he knew what type of situation he was in, Clint had an even better idea of who he was dealing with. It hadn't taken him long to pin down what kind of woman Kimberly was, and he knew for a fact that she would have come to find him later that night anyway. Now that he made it clear she was in his sights as well, she would back off and wait for him to come running back.

Walking around the front of the house, Clint waited and listened just in case Kimberly decided to follow him right then and there. If she was the type of person he thought she was, she was more interested in the chase than the actual goal. Most people who chose to live their lives outside the law were like that. They were hunters and were only happy when they were on the prowl.

Sure, there were those thieves who just needed the money, or killers who had a grudge to satisfy, but those were the ones who ran once the job was done. Someone would have to have more experience and passion for their work to pull off the type of job being pulled on the Fischer ranch. Kimberly was one of those and Clint knew damn well how to deal with her. The biggest challenge was in seeing through the mask she'd been wearing. Fortunately, she was so cocky that she made that part rather easy.

Heading for the corner of the house, Clint kept his steps slow and steady and his ears waiting for the sound of a door opening or someone walking behind him. He heard neither, but just to be sure, he glanced behind him to take a quick look.

There were people about, but nobody nearby and no trace of Kimberly. Clint smiled and rounded the corner. It felt good to be on top of the situation, even if it was just for a little while.

Once he made it to the side of the house, Clint stepped up his pace until he was hustling toward the back at a quick jog. The guards were in sight, but too far away to see too many details so close to the house itself. Whatever they were after, it must have been awfully important to Mr. Fischer to keep them all so spread out.

Clint felt a stab of guilt for thinking of that silver-haired man as Mr. Fischer. He knew now that the man was an imposter, but Clint simply didn't know what else to call him. He just had to make sure not to do that when he was talking to Grace.

Keeping that in mind, Clint rounded the next corner and headed straight for the door that led into the kitchen.

THIRTY-NINE

Clint walked into the kitchen and couldn't see Grace anywhere. He started looking for the small door she'd been talking about, but stopped when he saw he was being watched by a pair of older women who were cleaning dishes and stacking them in the pantry.

Before he started giving the excuse he'd prepared, Clint was stopped by a raised hand from one of the cleaning women.

"Over there," the older woman said, pointing to a small door she'd been blocking with her own body. "She's waiting for you." Picking up on Clint's uneasiness, she added, "Don't worry about nobody finding you. I doubt anyone even cares where the food comes from, so they don't know where to look."

The second old woman gave a snorting laugh. "And we sure ain't about to tell them, either."

Clint tipped his hat. "Thanks, ladies. I appreciate it."

"Then show it by helping that poor young thing in there. She can't keep up her act for much longer before someone finds out who she is."

Rather than follow up with those two, Clint opened the door and stepped into a small room lit by a single candle.

That candle was in Grace's hand and she was sitting on the floor as though she'd been punished for something.

Her knees were pulled up tight against her chest, making her look even more like her little sister. She looked scared the moment the door opened, but relaxed a bit when she saw Clint step inside. "Close the door tight," she said. "That way nobody can hear us from the kitchen."

After pulling the door shut as far as it would go, Clint found a barrel along one wall and sat on it. "The other workers know about you?" he asked.

"Not all of them. Just the ones in the kitchen. My sister told them when they were first brought in by them others, and they kept the secret. They're not like those others. They're just regular folks who cook and clean. They was going to quit when they found out, but they're too scared about what might happen if they do."

Clint thought back to the look on the old women's faces. There was some wariness there to be sure, but there was some protectiveness as well. He doubted they were staying put just because they were scared. It made him feel good to know that at least someone had been looking after those girls.

"I can't be missing for too much longer, Grace. Please tell me what you know."

The girl took another breath and let it out slowly. "My poppa said there was trouble, and when he went to see what happened . . . I heard shots. After that, I didn't see him again. Mother told me and my sister to go and hide until she knew what was going on. We did, and she went outside to talk to some men who worked for my poppa.

"I was so scared, and it was so long before I heard anything else from mother. That's when I heard the men come into the house. They stormed in and were screaming and hollering for everyone to come out and show themselves. Some did and some didn't. The ones who didn't were screaming and running. I could hear them trying to get away. Then there was more shooting."

Although the words were flowing from her mouth, Grace looked as though she was barely conscious of it. She rattled through the speech with a faraway look in her eyes, fighting back the tears that came along with the memories.

Clint wanted to reach out and comfort her, but she seemed fragile enough huddled in her corner that he was afraid of startling her. Instead, he sat back and listened.

A tear broke loose and ran down her cheek. Grace wiped it away and continued with her story. "I heard the screaming and the shooting and I knew my mother and poppa were dead. I could feel it like my heart was hurting. I wanted to check on them, but my sister was crying and if I left her she might make noise. Or if I left her, I thought the men would find us and they would . . ." She trailed off and suddenly seemed to open her eyes. She looked around as though she'd just woken from a bad dream, and the tears started to flow from the corners of her eyes.

Clint reached out then and put his hands on her shoulders. He knew she would try to pull away, and he kept hold of her when she did. "Grace, look at me," he said with just enough sternness to catch her attention. "There was nothing you could have done. Understand? You were right to hide and keep your sister safe. Your parents were right to keep you hidden."

"But if I did something else, I might have—"

"You might have gotten hurt. And your sister might have gotten hurt." He paused to let that sink in. Although she was still crying, Grace wasn't shaking so much and was beginning to catch her breath. "If you tell me the rest of what happened, I can help you. Do you think you can talk some more now, or do you want to wait?"

After a few more shuddering breaths, Grace nodded and said, "I can talk now."

"Good. Now, what happened after the shooting stopped?"

FORTY

As Clint had hoped, the girl settled even more once she focused on the memories after all hell had broken loose. She was a long way from happy and healthy, but she wasn't about to fall apart either. Watching her pull herself together, Clint had to admire the kid's strength. There were plenty of adults without the guts she was showing just by surviving the ordeal she'd been describing.

"After the shooting was over, the other men came in and started going through the house," Grace said. "They yelled for anyone else to show themselves, but we hid anyway. After that, they started bringing more people in. There were more of the men with guns and some others that started taking away my family's things and setting up as though this was their house."

"They brought in new servants?" Clint asked, piecing the whole thing together in his mind.

"Yes. They cleared out all the pictures and personal things until there was only enough to fill half the rooms. I would go and check up on things when they were gone or asleep. I've gotten real good at being quiet.

"Anyway, all the workers that used to be here, all the helpers and cooks and such, were gone. There were new ones now and that's when Martha found me." Seeing the confusion on Clint's face, Grace smiled a bit and old him, "Martha is the lady standing outside the door with the green apron. She found me and my sister and took us as her own.

"She told the men that we were her nieces and that we worked with her. I guess nobody cared to check, since the men never even thought twice about it. I know Mother and Poppa are gone, but my sister doesn't. I think if I tell her, she'll fuss too much and make the men come for me and her."

Now that she'd finished talking, Grace looked as though she was about to collapse. The story had taken a lot out of her, and it had even had an effect on Clint. He'd known there was something else going on, but he had no idea it would turn out like this.

The man claiming to be Mr. Fischer sounded like a man obsessed with his land, but Clint never would have figured he'd gotten that land by rolling in and taking over another man's home and property. He'd even taken on the Fischer name and swept out all reminders of the people who that name truly belonged to.

The more he thought about it, the sicker Clint felt.

"I want you to find your sister and get her someplace safe," Clint said. "Take her to the best hiding spot you know. After that, spread the word to anyone else who isn't one of the people who took away this house from you and your parents. Are there many like that?"

"Just the workers and the liveryman. Everyone else was shooting and yelling the night my parents were taken away. I know because I saw their faces through a crack in the wall."

Clint stopped her there, before she could say another word. "That hiding place you told me about. Is this it?"

Grace shook her head.

"Good. Don't tell me where it is. That way, nobody can find you."

"How will I know when to come out?"

"You said you could see through a crack in the wall. Could you hear things as well?"

"Yes. I could hear the men shouting."

"Good. When it's safe, I'll shout for you. This part is important, Grace. If you hear me shout the horses are running, that means everything is all right. That way, you know it's really me and that everything is really safe. If you don't hear me say the horses are running, you and everyone else need to stay put and stay quiet. Understand?"

Grace nodded.

"What will I say if everything is safe?"

"The horses are running."

"Good. Remember that and do what I said."

She stood up as if to leave, but stopped in front of Clint. "What if I don't hear you?"

"You will. When it's safe, I'll shout for you until you come, and then I'll look for you and never stop until I find you."

"What if . . . what if something happens to you? Like it happened to my parents?"

"It won't, Grace. I promise. I might be gone for a while, but it won't be more than a day. I'll come back for you, your sister and everyone else. I swear, I will. Just round everyone up and hide as soon as you can."

"But they'll be expecting dinner in a few hours."

"Don't worry. In a few hours, they'll all have a lot more on their minds than eating dinner."

"Will there . . ." Grace stopped and clenched her lips shut tight. Turning away from him, she reached out for the door and then stopped again. The girl looked over her shoulder at Clint and spoke again in a steady voice. "Will there be more shooting?"

After steeling himself and getting up from his makeshift seat, he said, "Yeah, Grace. There's going to be more shooting."

FORTY-ONE

Clint followed Grace out of the pantry and headed through the kitchen to the dining room. From there, he made a straight line for the front door, and before he could reach for the handle, the door began to open on its own. He knew who was going to be there and wasn't the least bit surprised to find Kimberly staring back at him.

"My, you look like you're just full of fire," she said.

Clint put on a smile and walked past her onto the front porch. "I was just looking for you," he said.

"Well, you've found me. And here I thought I was going to have to sit through a whole night by myself."

"I couldn't wait that long. And don't tell me you seriously thought I could."

Smiling victoriously, Kimberly reached out and ran both hands along Clint's arms. "I didn't think that for a second. My father's looking for you."

"Is he?"

She nodded. "Yes, he is. And I'm supposed to bring you to him as soon as I find you."

"Something tells me you're not the type of girl who is bossed around so easily. Just because he ordered you to look for me, that doesn't mean you have to find me right away. At least, you don't have to tell him you found me."

Looking into his eyes, she pressed herself against him and purred when she felt Clint's hands roaming up and down her back. "What are you suggesting?"

"I want to help your father hunt down this man, but I need to ask a few questions. It's something you might be able to help me with more than him."

"What kind of questions?"

"A better description. Things he might have said while his guard was down. People say things in front of women that they might not say in front of anyone else."

Her grin turned into something a little more conniving when she heard that. Kimberly looked as though she found something Clint said to be funny in a way that only she would understand. Fortunately, that was exactly the kind of reaction Clint had been hoping for.

"Men do act strangely in front of women sometimes. They all let their guard down sooner or later."

"That's what I wanted to talk about, but it should only take a little while. How about some time to ourselves?"

Obviously enjoying the verbal dance that she was certain she was leading, Kimberly put on a thin veil of hesitancy. "You can ask your questions here."

Clint let out a strained breath and held her a little tighter. "I'm still thinking about what you did in my room. I can't stop thinking about what I wanted to do to you. Even if it's just for a moment, I need to get you somewhere quiet. I'm sure I can keep you busy once I ask my questions."

"But I'm not the only one looking for you. If someone sees me talking to you, they might get the wrong idea."

Clint leaned down so that his lips brushed against Kimberly's ear when he whispered to her. "Then you'll have to take me somewhere nobody else will be looking, so I can have you all to myself."

Her head snapped away from him, and for a moment

Clint thought that she was getting suspicious of this sudden change of plans. She looked over his shoulder and then glanced around the land in front of the house. There was increasing activity, but many of the riders were still too far out to be able to know that Clint was the shape standing on the porch.

"Come on," Kimberly said, taking Clint by the hand and rushing off toward the livery. "I know a place, but we can't stay there too long."

Clint allowed himself to be dragged toward the livery. Kimberly turned sharply before getting too close to the stable and headed for, another smaller building instead.

"This used to be another stable," she told him. "But now it's just used for storage. We can talk in here."

The smaller building had to have been a carriage house or even a place where other animals were kept. There was straw littering the floor, and it had the smell of a barn. Keeping Grace's story in mind, Clint looked around and saw that the place seemed a little too empty.

Much like the study, there were places on the floor and walls that had been cleared off as if there had once been something there. Sections of the floor were free of straw and litter, revealing empty squares of wood floor. Pegs were arranged on the walls as if tools and equipment were supposed to be hanging there.

At the moment, the building carried nothing but straw and a pair of wagon wheels. Kimberly led him over to those wheels and leaned against the wall beside them.

"So here we are," she said. "What did you want to ask me?"

Clint leaned forward and placed his hands against the wall on either side of her head. Trapping her there, he let the silence continue before moving his face in close to hers. "What happened between you and Mark Tanner?"

"He said he was a dangerous man. That's why he was hired."

"And you like dangerous men, don't you?"

Her eyes widened for a second, and she pulled in a quick, excited breath. "Yes."

Clint mimicked the excited, victorious smile that he'd seen on her face only moments ago and leaned in to kiss her gently on the neck. Working his way up from there, he waited until he was nibbling on her earlobe to say, "I like hearing you say that."

She started to say something, but her words were forgotten as Clint's hand wandered over her waist and then down to her thigh. Her eyes clenched shut when she felt him touch her between her legs, his fingers moving and probing as though her skirt wasn't even there.

She moved her legs apart for him, then clenched him tightly as he massaged her. "Yes," she whispered. "Oh, yes."

FORTY-TWO

Reaching around to hold Kimberly's backside, Clint lifted her up off her feet and felt one of her legs wrap tightly around him. He used his other hand to pull up her skirt and slip, pushing beneath the material until he could feel the smooth, warm skin that was underneath. She was still moaning softly in his ear, squirming against him as he moved his hand up along her leg.

Clint allowed himself to fall into the heat of the moment, even though he had his own plans as to where that moment was headed. It seemed fitting for him to use the tactic on her, especially since Kimberly was surely planning to use it against him.

For the moment, however, Clint thought of nothing but the feel of her body and the warmth between her legs. That was almost enough to put him in the proper frame of mind, but then Kimberly herself began to help him when she reached down to slide her fingers between his legs.

"These have got to go," she said while undoing his jeans. Kimberly put both feet on the ground just long enough for her to pull his pants down and reach in to stroke his hardening cock. Feeling him get harder in re-

sponse to her touch, she purred, "Mmmm, that's much
better."

With a little hop, she was back in his arms with both
legs wrapped around his waist. She spread her knees as
wide as she could, which allowed Clint to get so close
that the heat from their bodies bled right through the
clothes they bothered to keep on.

Now that her skirts were hiked up around her waist,
Clint could reach between her legs and feel that Kimberly
hadn't been wearing any undergarments whatsoever.
"You were ready for me, weren't you?"

She smiled wickedly. Pressing her shoulders against the
wall, Kimberly gave herself just enough room to reach
down and slide her fingertips over Clint's shaft. "I've been
ready for you since I heard you were coming to help us
with our little problem. I've heard about you, but didn't
think all the stories were true."

"What do you think now?"

Shifting her weight slightly, Kimberly guided him into
her and let out a breath as he slid all the way in. "I think
I was a fool to walk out of your room before." She leaned
her head back and closed her eyes, savoring the feel of
Clint thrusting in and out of her. "I want you to do this
to me all day and night."

Clint was savoring the moment as well. She was a
woman who knew how to use her body and wasn't
ashamed to do just that. He could see her giving in to the
pleasure she was feeling, just as he could feel her muscles
relaxing. She was letting him hold her now and allowing
him to make love to her.

Before, it had been her in charge. Now Kimberly was
being controlled, and Clint knew he was the one holding
the reins.

"Did Mark Tanner ever do this to you?" he asked.

"God, no. Mark never made me feel like this."

Clint grabbed onto her buttocks a little harder, which

caused her to tense for a moment and let out a passionate groan. "What about the man who lived here before? Did he get you alone like this?"

She smiled and was raking her nails across Clint's back. He was pumping into her more forcefully, banging her against the wall until it was all she could do to keep from screaming out his name. Her breaths were coming hard and ragged, but she finally managed to let out a rasping laugh.

"Not that one," she said. "He wanted me, but was too scared to—" Suddenly, her eyes snapped open, and she looked at Clint with pure shock. "What did you say?"

Slowing down his pace, Clint pressed himself against her breast and leaned forward so he could whisper directly into her ear. His hips had slowed down slightly, but hadn't stopped. Instead, he used slow, grinding circles while moving inside her.

"You heard me," he said.

"This is Mr. Fischer's place," she said. "There wasn't anyone here before." Kimberly pulled in a quick breath as she felt Clint drive all the way inside of her.

"You're starting to slip," he told her. "What's the matter? You don't seem used to being the one with their guard down."

Now there was some fear showing in her eyes, and she dropped her feet to the ground. "Let me go. Right now."

Clint backed up and pulled on his clothes while Kimberly straightened herself as quickly as she could. Once her skirts were down and covering her, she started to try and head for the door. Clint stopped her by holding his arm out in front of her and slamming his hand against the wall.

"Not so fast," he said. "I want to hear about what's really going on here."

"I don't know anything. Mr. Fi—My father is trying to

hunt down that man who hurt me and that's all there is to it."

Shaking his head, Clint said, "It's too late for all that. The least you could do is give me some credit for having a brain in my head. It's bad enough that you and Fischer's stories don't match, but then you slip up right now and expect me to forget about it."

"I didn't slip up."

"Is he your father or Mr. Fischer? No child makes that mistake when talking about someone so familiar. At least you didn't slip up even more and mention the man's real name."

Clint was watching her like a hawk, waiting to spot any change in her expression or manner. When he said that last part, her eyes widened for a second and her breath caught in the back of her throat.

"That's right," Clint said with a slow nod. "I know he's not Mr. Fischer, and that sure as hell makes you someone besides Kimberly Fischer. Start talking now, because this whole thing's set to come crashing down."

"All I have to do is start screaming and they'll shoot you down."

"And all I have to do is draw and put a bullet into you before you get me killed." In a flash of motion, Clint's hand dropped to his Colt, but he didn't clear leather. "I'll bet I can hit you from here. What do you think?"

She thought about it for less than a second before turning and leaning against the wall next to his hand. "What do you want to know?"

FORTY-THREE

"Who's this man who says he's Mr. Fischer?" Clint asked. He could tell that she wasn't about to run, but he still knew better than to take his hand away from his gun.

"Dave Winsloe. That's his real name."

"And I suppose your first name really is Kimberly?"

She nodded. "Easier to remember that way."

"So you and Dave and the rest of these men came across this spread and thought you might as well take it for yourselves? You just figured on wiping out all the workers and anyone else who might know, so you could just step right on in. Is that about right?"

Amazingly enough, Kimberly looked at him as though she was genuinely offended. "We knew what we were doing. We're not stupid. Me and Dave have been watching this place and a few others for months. We chose this one because the owner keeps to himself and uses other workers to make deliveries or buy things from town. And even when we started a couple minor problems, he never went to the law."

"You tested him?"

"Just some little things," she answered with a shrug. "Stealing a few horses and knocking down some fences.

Things like that. He always handled it on his own, using his own men. He thought he was the only law. It was perfect."

Despite the fact that what he heard was making Clint's stomach churn, he knew he had to hear it, and he didn't let his discomfort show to the woman doing the talking. "So how did this all start?"

Now that she thought she wasn't about to die, Kimberly allowed some of her previous attitude to creep back into her voice and expression. Whenever her nervous shifting got too far, however, she was put in her place by a warning glance from Clint. "I met up with the owner, got to know him and his wife." Putting on a wicked smirk, she added, "I got to know *him* better, though."

"Go on."

"I'd meet him right here and he'd fuck me all night long. I don't think that wife of his was doing the job. While he was busy, Dave would scout around the spread, and after I was done with the owner, I'd do more scouting of my own.

"This place only had about five or six men looking after it. We rode in here and were moving our things in the next day. It was easy."

"Shooting a man, his family and all his workers was pretty easy, huh? Was it so easy listening to the children scream for their parents?"

Clint watched for a reaction, but didn't get much of anything from Kimberly. She shrugged a little, which nearly got more of a reaction from him. Rather than follow through on the anger he was starting to feel toward her, Clint kept himself in check and said, "You're a hell of a lot colder than I expected."

"You've got to be in this business. It's all about making fools of people. That's the way to get rich. People are fools, and it's only too easy to make them slip up."

"Yeah. Right until you're the one slipping up."

Kimberly looked down at her feet. When she looked up again, she was wearing the same sexy grin that she'd been wearing all the other times Clint had seen her. "Maybe, but even you've got to admit we fit pretty well together. Don't tell me I didn't make you feel good."

"Sure, I'll admit it. You know what felt even better, though? Seeing you become the one who's on the receiving end of a con. Watching you slip up when your guard was down. Now, that felt good."

The smile dropped away from her face, and she clenched her lips together as though she was about to spit. Even so, she didn't have any way to come back from Clint's taunt.

"Who's Mark Tanner?" he asked.

"He's new to the group. He signed on for some smaller jobs and then started getting cold feet once we rode in to take over this place. I let him fuck me, too, but I swear he started to fall in love with me. He decided to head off on his own, took what he could and then made off with enough to bury Dave for good."

"What did he get?"

Kimberly shrugged her shoulders. "I don't know. All I know is what I heard from Dave. He said Mark rode off with a shipment, some money and something that might have buried us all. It doesn't matter, though. Dave got rid of whatever he was so worried about. All that's left is Mark, and he's probably dead already."

"I wouldn't count on that. Besides, you all have a lot more to worry about now."

"Is that so?" Kimberly said in a taunting voice. "And what's that?"

Clint leaned forward until he'd backed her all the way against the wall. Locking his eyes onto hers, he snarled, "You need to worry about me."

FORTY-FOUR

Between the miscellaneous scraps laying around the coach house and strips of Kimberly's own clothing, Clint had more than enough material to tie the woman up and gag her. Just to be sure, he made his way over to the livery and found some rope which he used to lash her to one of the wagon wheels in the small shack.

With her off his list of worries, Clint was ready to face some of the others. That nagging sensation in his gut was worse than ever, telling him that he needed to make his move and make it fast. All he needed was his eyes to know that much, since most of the men who'd been patrolling the grounds were now heading in from the outer perimeter.

Dave Winsloe was flanked by a pair of men, and all three of them were riding toward the front of the house. As soon as he spotted Clint, Winsloe steered his horse toward him, and the other two men followed suit. When he got a little closer, it was obvious that only one of the men at Dave's side was a guard. The other didn't seem too happy at all to be there.

"There you are, Mr. Adams!" Winsloe shouted. "Looks

like I put you up and fed you for nothing. Look at what my best tracker found."

Clint had already seen Winsloe's prize acquisition. That prize was the man riding on the horse next to the silver-haired fellow. And that man was Mark Tanner, tied up in much the same way that Clint had tied up Jonah at the end of their last meeting.

"You'll notice he's not gagged," Winsloe pointed out. "That's because Mark here has had a whole lot to say."

Just then, Clint noticed that Tanner's face was flushed and smeared with blood. There were cuts on his cheeks and a dark, blackened hole where his left eye had once been. After that amount of torture, Lord only knew what Tanner had said.

Winsloe pulled his horse to a stop ten feet in front of Clint and swung down from the saddle. "It took a little persuasion, of course, but Mark had plenty to say once he got going. He mentioned something about you talking to him way back when I'd asked you to track him down. Is that true? I mean, why would you do something like that when you were helping me?"

"It's true," Clint said. "Unlike everything else you've been telling me, Mr. Fischer. Or would it be easier to call you Mr. Winsloe?"

Although the silver-haired man didn't look overly surprised, he was at a loss for words. He stared down at Clint, nodding to himself until finally he said, "You know, Jonah said you'd be trouble. Too bad he couldn't get the job done the first time, or I wouldn't have had to deal with this now. Personally, I was hoping you'd look around a bit, eat some of my food and be on your way."

"And Kimberly was what? Entertainment? Why the whole story with her as your daughter?"

Winsloe shrugged. "It sounded good at the time. Whatever it took to get you on board."

"How long did you think this would last?" Clint asked.

"Did you seriously think you could live some other man's life?"

"Only until I sell off all his land and livestock. It's been done before. And it's not as hard as you might think. You only get in trouble once your own men betray you. Isn't that right, Mark? Taking off with those servants I missed wasn't very nice."

Tanner swayed in his saddle. Even trying to open his mouth brought a pained wince to his face.

Winsloe looked over his shoulder as a few more of his men came riding in toward the house. "Guess I'll have to do this the messy way. That is unless you'd rather come in with me, Mr. Adams? There's just one of the old servants out there that we need to find, and then we can bleed this place dry. Should be a hefty profit in it for everyone. What do you say?"

Taking in the scene around him, Clint counted half a dozen men that were close enough to be of any immediate concern and that was apart from Winsloe and the man riding beside him. Looking over to the silver-haired figure, Clint squared his shoulders and said, "I think it's going to have to be the messy way."

"So be it." Before he'd even finished speaking those words, Winsloe snapped his fingers and pulled back on his reins. "Kill him!" he shouted while turning his horse around toward the house.

The man who'd been riding as Winsloe's guard was already drawing his weapon. He'd gotten the pistol halfway from its holster by the time Clint turned his attention toward him and went for his Colt. Clint's hand moved like a flicker of lightning, and in less time than it took to blink, the modified gun was in his grasp.

The Colt barked once before the other man's hammer could drop, sending a bullet through the air and into the other man's forehead. His head snapped back and his body toppled from his horse. One foot came clear of the stirrups, but the other was wedged in tight, preventing the man from dropping out completely. His eyes were already glazed over as he hung upside down from the side of his horse.

More shots cracked through the air and the rumble of approaching horses was getting closer. Clint had already picked out the closest riders and was heading for the livery, which offered his best chance of cover. Lead smacked into the doors and wall of the stable as Clint dove through the big front door. He rolled once and hopped right back up to his feet with the Colt in hand.

As soon as he was able to catch his breath, Clint heard a couple horses coming to a halt not too far from the livery's entrance. He poked his head out to see how many had arrived, and it was only Clint's sharpened reflexes that allowed him to pull back again before the crackle of gunfire once again filled the air.

Clint knew that plenty more were on the way and waiting even for another couple seconds would only allow the gunmen to strengthen their forces. With that in mind, he took a breath and threw himself into a forward roll which ended up with him on one knee facing three gunmen still trying to track his movement with their eyes.

The Colt bucked against Clint's palm twice in quick succession, drilling holes through one man's chest and another's stomach. The man hit in the chest let out a grunt and dropped. The other two were already starting to return fire.

If one factor was to decide if a man was going to make it through a gunfight or not, it would have to be that man's ability to keep his wits about him. More important than speed, keeping a level head had seen Clint through more scrapes than he could count.

Both of the remaining two standing in front of Clint were plenty fast and had drawn their guns. They even got to fire, but they were too flustered to hit their target. The man hit in the gut sent his shot straight into the ground a couple feet in front of Clint. The third man got close enough to send a bullet hissing past Clint's ear, but it missed all the same.

His hand had already been tracking toward the third shooter, so Clint squeezed off a round at him. The bullet punched the man in the chest, spinning him around like a top. Clint took a moment to get to his feet and that was all the gut-shot man needed to take aim yet again.

Clint looked over to the man clutching his stomach, just as that one's pistol was about to go off. Without having to think about it, Clint finished him off with a round through the heart and then gave the third man a matching wound just to be sure.

There were more riders approaching, but Clint started walking calmly toward the house. "Winsloe!" he shouted while reloading the Colt. "Show yourself and I can take you in to the law. I guarantee you'd rather face them than me."

Winsloe stuck his head around from the front porch and took a quick shot which came nowhere near hitting Clint. "There isn't any law around here! And you're too out-gunned to be making threats like that, Mr. Adams."

Clint kept walking until he could see the front of the house. Winsloe was standing with his back pressed against a window, looking back at Clint down the barrel of his pistol. A smile drifted onto Winsloe's face as more riders pulled up and stopped once they'd gotten inside of firing range.

"You're surrounded, Mr. Adams. There's no law that can save you now."

FORTY-FIVE

Clint counted ten men spreading out around the front of the house. Winsloe made eleven, and he stood on that front porch as though he was at the head of an army.

"Jonah!" Winsloe shouted. "Come up here and finish off Mr. Adams here. I'd say you earned the honor."

One of the riders came forward and Clint immediately recognized the big man's face. Jonah had his gun out already and was sighting down the barrel when Clint snapped the Colt's cylinder shut and took a shots from the hip.

That shot whipped through the air and caught Jonah in the center of his chest, knocking him from the saddle as though he'd been hit by a club. Clint was already moving after that, fully expecting all hell to break loose. He wasn't disappointed.

All the other men started to fire, but they were just shooting in Clint's direction while trying to keep their horses under control. Some of the shots got close, but not enough to put a dent in Clint's resolve. He was in the fight and there was no getting out before it was over. Once a man came to that conclusion, there was precious little on earth that could shake him.

Suddenly, the amount of gunfire seemed to double. Then, it tripled, followed by the sound of shattering glass.

At first, Clint thought Winsloe's men were turning their fire toward the house. Then he realized that the next wave of gunshots were actually coming from the house. Once his shoulder was pressed against the nearest wall, Clint could feel the reverberation of frenzied steps along with the rumble of shot after shot coming from inside.

A pair of Winsloe's men charged around the corner and Clint shot them down out of sheer instinct. He held the Colt as though he was pointing his finger, sending a bullet into each of the oncoming gunmen. They jerked back as the lead tore through them, landing on the ground to move no more.

Clint looked around at the other men that had been after him and saw three bodies laying in the dirt that he hadn't put there. Bullets hissed through the air beside him, cutting into the few remaining gunmen that were dumb enough to stay in range. One of them caught a round between the shoulders and fell as the rest managed to take off in all directions.

Waiting until the shots died down, Clint chanced a look through the nearest broken window and saw a familiar face looking down the barrel of an older model rifle.

"Martha?" Clint asked.

The old woman nearly fired into his face at point-blank range, but recognized him before pulling her trigger. "Mr. Adams. You're alive. Praise the lord."

"What's going on here? Where did you get those guns?"

Just then, the front door swung open and a man stepped outside. He had the shape of a man and walked like a man, but looked more like something that had been buried beneath a tree stump for ten years and was only recently dug up again. "They're Mr. Fischer's guns. The real Mr. Fischer. I gave them out to the servants."

"And who are you?"

"I'm Alex Wright."

"The man Mark Tanner was looking for?"

The man nodded. "Me and some of the other folks who used to work for the Fischers were ambushed on our way out. Mark tried to get us out of here so I could tell the sheriff in Sharpeston everything that's happened. We were the only ones left who knew enough to prove that he wasn't who he was claiming to be."

Looking down at Winsloe, who was cowering on the porch with his arms over his head, Wright said, "That one there killed the workers he could find and burnt their bodies so nobody could even recognize them. He said we knew enough to bury him and his whole crew. Maybe he was right." As he said that, the rifle in his hand came up to point into Winsloe's face.

As far as Clint could tell, Winsloe was only still alive because he'd dropped down beneath the windows as all the gunshots flew over him. It also looked as though Winsloe wasn't able to move under his own power.

"So what do you think?" Clint asked the silver-haired man who now looked about one second away from messing his pants. "You ready to face the law now?"

Winsloe squinted up at Clint and gritted his teeth. "Fuck you," he spat as he lifted his weapon to aim at Clint.

Before Clint could react, one more shot blasted through the air. It sounded like a clap of thunder because it came from the gun held by Alex Wright.

Wright's shot cleared a path through Winsloe's skull. "That's the only law he deserves," Wright said before letting the gun fall from his fingers.

Clint stepped forward and helped Wright move inside. The other man looked as though he could barely walk and was having trouble catching his breath. "I owe you one hell of a thank-you," Clint said after showing Wright to a chair. "When did you arrange all of this?"

Wright was pale, but it seemed to do him some good to talk. "I just got back an hour or so ago. I've been running ever since the wagon was ambushed. I wasn't sure if Tanner set us up or not, so I wasn't about to meet up with him.

"When I got back, I heard that you were here and meant to help. I knew Mr. Fischer had some guns to arm his men in case there was any trouble, so I handed them out to whoever I could. Seems like these folks weren't all too happy about working for those killers either."

Looking around, Clint saw the faces of all the servants he'd met since he'd gotten to the ranch. Even the livery-man was there, his face smudged by dirt and gunpowder.

"We may have worked for them," the liveryman said. "But we ain't killers. There just was no way for us to break away from 'em, that's all."

Clint nodded and patted the liveryman on the shoulder. "I doubt you'll ever see those men again. The ones that are left will be scattered and desperate to get away from here. But I hope you all have somewhere to go, just the same."

"Mr. Fischer's horses are still here," Wright said. "I'm sure he wouldn't mind if we used them now. Him and his wife . . . they were good people. They would have wanted us to be safe."

Clint nodded, thinking about how long it would take for him to round up the rest of Winsloe's men before they tried invading another home. It was hard to say, but he figured he could track most of them down in a few days. He was certain he'd come across the others over time. Men like that always had a knack for catching up to him.

At that moment, a bit of movement caught Clint's eye. He turned and looked into a pair of faces that were frightened, yet beautiful at the same time. They were grateful, as well. Very, very grateful.

Standing behind her little sister with both hands on the smaller girl's shoulders, Grace Fischer looked at Clint and said, "The horses are running."

Watch for

THE DEVIL'S SPARK

262nd novel in the exciting GUNSMITH series
from Jove

Coming in October!

**Explore the exciting Old West with one
of the men who made it wild!**